Sherlock Holmes, The Adventure of the Grinning Cat

By Joseph W. Svec III

Paperback ISBN 9781780928852
ePub ISBN 9781780928869
PDF ISBN 9781780928876

Published in the UK by MX Publishing
335 Princess Park Manor, Royal Drive,
London, N11 3GX
www.mxpublishing.com

Cover design by www.staunch.com

The author may be contacted via his web page,
www.pixymuse.com or via his Facebook page
www.facebook.com/sherlockgrinningcat

Dedication

This book is dedicated to my loving, magical and gifted wife, Lidia. Thank you for your continued encouragement and traveling this curious and enjoyable journey with me.

Acknowledgements:

I would like to acknowledge and thank the following wonderful people for their assistance in making this book possible.

First I would like to thank my wife Lidia for listening to each chapter as it was completed and providing excellent suggestions and encouragement during the writing of this book.

I would like to thank my son Joe for introducing me to the Amador County Holmes' Hounds Sherlockian Society which provided my first exposure to the adventures of Sherlock Holmes.

I would like to thank my daughter Leedia for listening to a reading of this book and providing comments.

Thank you very much to Linda Hein and Beth Barnard for reviewing the manuscript, and providing most valuable input. It is very much appreciated.

Thank you to the Amador County Holmes' Hounds Sherlockian Society and Baker Street West of Jackson California for excellent inspiration.

Table of Contents:

A Note to Readers:

The following manuscript and cover letter was found in the belongings of Dr. John Watson, M.D. after he passed away in the early 1900s. You may recall that besides being a war veteran and a well respected surgeon, Dr. Watson was also noted for being the close friend and biographer of Sherlock Holmes, the world famous consulting detective. Dr. Watson recorded the more interesting and challenging of Sherlock Holmes' many cases and adventures propelling him into the spotlight.

Sherlock Holmes was world renowned for his uncanny skills in perception, logic and deductive reasoning, as well his astute knowledge in many unique subject areas. He was especially noted for seeing the minute details that were invisible to everyone else. In addition to his solving the most baffling and difficult cases that vexed Scotland Yard he had also published numerous technical papers on a wide variety of arcane subjects, many of which are mentioned in this story.

Per Dr. Watson's written notes in the cover letter, this manuscript apparently was set aside for 25 years as he requested, but then was lost over the passing decades until it was recently rediscovered. As the requested time period has more than passed, it may now be published without concern and the reader may judge for his or herself. Be prepared for a very strange and most curious tale.

Prologue

Memorandum:

To: Whom It May Concern
From: Dr. John Watson M.D.
Subject: Sherlock Holmes, The Adventure of the Grinning
Cat
Date: February, 1898

First let me state unequivocally that the events described below really did happen. As utterly improbable or even impossible as they may seem to you as you read this, they actually did occur exactly as I have described them. I recorded the details of this very strange adventure almost as soon as it was complete so that I would not forget even one fantastical aspect of this amazing experience. If you have read my previous accounts of the great consulting detective, Sherlock Holmes, then you will see at once how utterly different this adventure is from each of his previous exploits. In all my years spent accompanying Sherlock Homes in his cases, I have never before experienced one like this. My mind still reels in wonder when I think back to it all.

Yet as true and real as it was, I must take Sherlock Holmes' advice and ask that its publication be postponed until 25 years after my passing. After all, I must consider my reputation as a medical practitioner as well as the confidence of my patients, not to mention the reputation of Sherlock Holmes himself. Upon reading this, it is entirely possible that one may question the sanity of the author. I must confess that I questioned my own sanity several times during the course of this adventure.

However, I must also ask that the reader refer to the rather odd newspaper article in the February 5, 1898, London Daily Times that is referenced within the manuscript, and then you may make your own judgment. Either way, your compliance in this request is greatly appreciated.

Dr. John H. Watson, M.D.

Sherlock Holmes,
The Adventure of the Grinning Cat

Chapter 1. A Very Strange Visitor (Now that's rather unusual.)

It was a cold and foggy February 4, 1898, rather typical for that time of year actually, but most untypically, Sherlock Holmes was not quite his usual self that day. No, not at all. Not in the least. And I must confess that even after all of the unusual and quite incredible adventures we had shared up until the morning of that very strange visitor, I was rather beside myself as well.

Countless times I had witnessed Holmes solving a multitude of odd and unusual cases without the slightest bit of hesitation or difficulty. He had applied his uncanny senses of observation, logic and deduction to disprove vampires, phantoms, demon dogs, and more. He had written volumes of scholarly papers on the most arcane and esoteric of subjects. Yet on that particular day, there he sat in deep concentration, just staring. Now this was not at all his normal mode of deep concentration in which he sat in silence puffing away incessantly on his pipe until the room was filled with noxious fog, or playing his violin until one's nerves cringed and one could not stand another shrieking, blood curdling note. No, this time he just sat there completely still as if in a trance and stared intently at the very strange visitor sitting in the chair across from him. Now, it is also very true that we had never before had a visitor or client quite like this, so I would imagine that Sherlock's behavior is somewhat understandable.

He had been staring at him, or should I say "it", since just after it appeared that morning in the study. We had come down for breakfast as usual only to find a cat sitting in the chair across from Sherlock's. It was a rather large cat with big green eyes and a grayish coat that suggested bluish black stripes.

"Hello? What's this? What are you doing here? How did you even get in here?" Sherlock wonderingly asked, never expecting a reply. But then the most unimaginable thing possible happened: The cat broke into a very wide grin and while gazing in the direction of the front door, replied, "Hello to yourself Sherlock Holmes. I am here to engage your services, and I came through that door".

We stood there rather shocked for a moment before I addressed Holmes asking, "Did that cat just talk to us?"

To which the cat turned and looked directly at Sherlock and replied while nodding its head in my direction, "Not very observant this one, is he? Or is he just hard of hearing? Now I know why you're the detective."

Sherlock broke into a wide grin himself and slapped me on the shoulder saying, "Good job Watson! After all these years, you have finally managed to pull one over on me. I really did not know you were into ventriloquism. How long have you been working at it? You did an excellent job you know! Just smashing! And how on Earth did you manage to get the cat in here? I was up rather late, and I locked the door myself last night. There were no cats here in the study when I went to sleep."

4

The grinning cat then jumped off the chair saying, "My dear Mr. Holmes, this has nothing at all to do with ventriloquism. Your friend Watson could not throw his voice even if he had a catapult." At which point its grin grew impossibly wider, and it laughed: "Get it? A 'catapult'?? I'm a cat??? Never mind. I know you are not noted for having a sense of humor. As I was saying, I came 'through' that door."

At that point, the cat casually walked towards and then completely through the solid wooden door vanishing right before our eyes. How in the world could it do that? Were we seeing things? I was about to ask Sherlock if he had seen the same thing I did, when there was a considerable amount of loud scratching on the other side of the door and we were able to hear a cat mewing outside of the door as well. However, before we could react, the cat's wide smile and piercing eyes appeared on the inner surface of the wooden door winking at us. This was immediately followed by the rest of its head (minus the body mind you!) reappearing on our side of the door, saying, "See? Like I told you, I came 'through' that door. I can do that, you know. We Cheshire Cats are noted for such things. "Seeing our shock, he added, "Really we are. I could do it again if you don't believe me."

It then continued coming 'through' the door, completed reforming the rest of its body, slowly crossed the room, taking particular care to rub itself several times against Sherlock's pants leg, leaving a good quantity of cat hair as it did, jumped back up on the chair, sat down and stared at us. Sherlock brushed the cat hair off of his leg, very carefully examining it with the hand microscope he had removed from his pocket. Although one might not expect it, Sherlock Holmes is quite the expert on cat hair. He had once written a monograph on the subject. I think it was titled: *Determining Human Disposition to Violent Behavior Based on the Nature and Quantity of Cat Hair on Clothing,* or something like that. Sherlock then crossed the room, slowly seated himself into his chair right across from it and commenced staring at the cat.

This had begun at about 7:00 am, and the clock was now already near 9:00 am. Nothing had been said; neither one had moved. They sat quietly staring at each other the whole time. Just out of curiosity, to answer a question that came to mind while I was waiting and observing, I had gotten up, opened the door, looked at the outside of it, verified the brand new scratch marks on the outer surface, closed the door, and sat down again. Now that I think about it, I recall Sherlock writing a paper on identifying scratch marks as well. I think it was called: *Identification and Classification of Mammalian Species Based on Scratch Marks on Wooden Doors.*

At one point, I had considered throwing a blanket over the cat to remove it from our sight, but just at the time that I was considering that, it turned and looked at me with its impossible grin as if to say, "Watson, you know that would not accomplish a thing. I would simply dematerialize and let the blanket pass right through me, re-materialize, and be sitting right here still waiting for Sherlock Holmes to say something."

But Holmes did not say a thing. He continued sitting there staring at the cat. I could almost see the gears and cogs of his analytical thinking process as he considered, reconsidered, analyzed, and then eliminated one explanation after another for our very strange visitor. I am sure each possibility was more bizarre than the previous.

Yet in his mind logic *must* prevail. There is always a simple explanation if one can get one past the confusing distractions. As Sherlock had admonished me so many times previously, "After eliminating the impossible, whatever remains, no matter how improbable, must be true."

Finally, close to 10:00 am, with a long deep sigh, he shook his head, stood up, went over to the breakfast table, poured a saucer of milk, apparently for the cat, poured for me and himself two cups of tea, brought them back into the study, and set them down. He looked at the cat intensely and said. "All right. Against all rational logic, probabilities and likelihoods and as completely strange as it may seem, you really *are* here. Have a bowl of milk. Now tell me, how can I possibly be of any help to you? I am sure you are not here to read my paper on *Malfunctions, Breakdowns and Misdirection in the Feline Homing Instinct.*"

Chapter 2. A Very Strange Tea Party (Now it's really getting unusual.)

The cat's grin softened somewhat as it looked towards the direction of the tea service and replied, "Actually, I would prefer some tea with that milk, if you don't mind." Turning back to Sherlock, it pointed out. "You know, it only took you three hours to eliminate all other possibilities and determine that, as completely improbable as it may seem, I truly am sitting right here in front of you. That is quite good. You really do live up to your reputation."

He turned, nodding in my direction and commented, "You could learn quite a lot from this one, Watson. You really must pay closer attention. However, it does appear that your stories of his exploits and adventures are not exaggerated in the slightest."

Then turning back to Sherlock the cat requested: "Well, you can start by adding some tea to my milk-- Earl Grey, if you have it-- pouring two more cups of tea, and answering the door." At which point there immediately commenced a loud thumping at the door. While Holmes went to get the additional tea, I strode towards the door, opened it and found myself, if at all possible, even more dumbfounded than I already had been with the day's proceedings. For, there before me standing upright on its hind legs, was a large white rabbit wearing a blue waistcoat and holding a large gold pocket watch in his paw, asking repeatedly, "Are we late? Are we late? Oh, I do hope we are not too late!"

Standing beside him stood an extremely short and oddly dressed fellow with shocking red hair, and an enormous brightly colored top hat on his head that was almost as tall as its wearer, and an equally large polka-dotted bow tie. With a grand flourish and much waving of his hands, he bowed as he introduced himself and his companion: "The Hatter, at your service." Straightening up, and reversing the flourish of his hands so that they ended up pointing towards his companion, he very formally stated, "Allow me to present Mr. White Rabbit, Esquire." At which point the White Rabbit again implored, "Please tell me we are not too late! Are we too late??? I really do hope we are not too late! I don't know what we would do if we were too late!"

Felling completely confused, looking back and forth between them, I bewilderedly replied, "No, I don't think so. Late for what exactly? I am not quite certain or sure about anything at this point."

"That's wonderful!" cried the Hatter, as he followed by the White Rabbit marched past me into the room. "That makes two of us. You know that I am never *really* quite certain or sure of anything myself, except Tea Time of course, so I do think I could possibly use a cup of tea right about now. Yes, that would probably be most lovely."

I closed the door behind them and wondered how the ever-so-logical-and-grounded-in-reality, Sherlock Holmes would respond to these new and even more bizarre visitors. They were certainly much stranger than the cat that was sitting there. But having already given the cat some tea to go with his milk, and holding a cup of tea in each hand, he looked at them and calmly asked, "Does the

Reverend Charles Dodgson, better known by his pen name, Lewis Carroll know that you three are here?"

"That's the problem!" they all three exclaimed at once. "Or least that's the second half of the problem," said the cat, "Lewis Carroll is missing!"

All three commenced to vigorous nodding, agreeing and bemoaning the fact that Lewis Carroll was indeed missing, and that it was most assuredly the second half of their very serious problem. Holmes held up his hand to gain their attention and get the conversation back under some semblance of control if that was at all possible, and asked them, "So tell me please, what exactly is the *first half* of the problem? You do know I wrote a paper once on *Analysis, Determination, Division and Classification of Issues in the Hierarchy of Problem Identification and Resolution.*"

"Alice is missing from Wonderland!" they all exclaimed together, then adding, "And so is the March Hare! Where can they be? What *are* we to do?" And once again they commenced to nodding at each other lamenting, agreeing and wondering what on earth or in Wonderland could possibly be done. The cat again interjected. "That's why we came to see you, Mr. Holmes. After all, you are known as the world's foremost consulting detective this side of Wonderland, and we really don't have any consulting detectives on that side of Wonderland. And besides, even if we did have, they too would have probably vanished by now. You simply must help us find Alice and the others before we disappear as well. All of Wonderland depends on you!"

Holmes gestured for the new guests to sit down, handed

them cups of tea and slowly asked them, "Why don't you tell me your story and start at the beginning, when you first noticed something strange going on?" Looking at the three of them and considering the peculiarity of the situation, he paused for a moment, and added, "Or at least stranger than a talking cat that can dematerialize, a talking rabbit in blue waist coat and...," Once again, Holmes hesitated, looking directly at the Hatter who smiled at Holmes raising his tea cup in a salute. Sherlock nodded his head and raised his tea cup in return and concluded, "And him, who I am at a loss to describe."

All three looked at one another for only a moment glancing back and forth and once again began talking and gesturing all at once until Holmes again held up his hand and interjected, "If you please! One speaker at a time!"

The Cheshire Cat taking the lead and gesturing towards The Hatter, stated rather matter-a-factly, "Since I am a cat, and you know that cats can never be entirely trusted, and he's mad as a hatter, which is to be completely expected since he is one, why don't you explain it to him Rabbit? You know that rabbits are considered to be quite trustworthy, as well as very cute and cuddly, and after all, it did all begin when Alice followed you down the rabbit hole."

The Rabbit shied backward with a look of surprised indignation exclaiming, "Cute and cuddly? I am certainly not cute or cuddly! I am m-most assuredly distinguished looking and I paid dearly for it. Do you know what this jacket cost? I assure you, Cheshire, no one thinks of m-m-me as cute or cuddly! Cute and cuddly indeed!" Then realizing that everyone in the room was staring at him, he

11

cleared his throat, looked around rather nervously, straightened up, and began his unusual tale.

Chapter 3. A Very Strange Tale (Can it get any more unusual than this?)

"A-a-actually, I think it may have begun when Lewis Carroll took that boat ride with Alice Liddell and her sisters and first told them about Wonderland. Or perhaps it began when he wrote it all down for her. It could have been something in the ink or the paper, or m-m-maybe it was just his will to create that somehow brought Wonderland and all of its inhabitants to life. M-m-maybe even Alice and her cats as well since they are part of the stories. I really don't know for certain. All we know is that since that day when she first visited Wonderland, we have been truly alive. We have been living in Alice's Wonderland adventures along with her and continuing living on each day in between Alice's visits and adventures.

"It has not been just her adventures down the rabbit hole and through the looking glass, but her newer adventures as well. Sir, you can't imagine the noise from all of those musical instruments playing at the same time when Alice visited Orchestra Land. And that trip she took to the m-m-moon? Why that was really incredible! I m-must say though, I enjoyed that cheese she brought back from the m-moon. I know some people have said the m-m-moon is m-made of cheese, but I never really believed it for m-myself until I tasted it. Have you ever tasted green cheese from the m-m-moon sir? It really is quite delicious. Now some of her adventures I unfortunately did m-miss because I was a bit too late, but we did have so many wonderful adventures together, all of us. Oh, I do hope we are not too late. Are we too late M-Mr. Holmes?"

As his ears twitched repeatedly, the Rabbit glanced nervously at his watch, took a deep breath, and then continued. "One day, Alice just disappeared from Wonderland. That is to say, she did not show up for our regular Wednesday afternoon tea. And I m-must tell you sir, Alice never m-m-misses tea! She is always there precisely on Wednesday afternoon for tea. Why, if my watch kept dates instead of time, I could set my watch by her. We have such lovely tea parties, all of us together. Every Wednesday..."

Standing up and striking a formal public speaking pose, the Hatter interjected, "Rabbit, you have most certainly established that Alice was regularly there for tea on Wednesdays. What happened next? We may not have much time left."

Glancing at his watch in fear, the Rabbit continued. "Three weeks ago, Alice did not show up for Wednesday afternoon tea as usual. We thought that m-m-maybe she had been caught up in a game of chess or a Wonderland croquet m-m-match, or something. M-Mr. Holmes, do you know how challenging it can be playing croquet with flamingos for m-mallets, hedge hogs for croquet balls, and wickets that get up and switch their positions on you?"

Sherlock shook his head sideways and replied, "No, I can't say that I do. But I did once write a magazine article on *The Logic and Geometry of Lining up Croquet Shots for Maximum Efficiency*. But as I recall, the wickets involved were all quite stationary."

The Rabbit gestured widely, pointing his paws all over the room, "What with the wickets continuously getting up, running around, switching their positions and charging all over the croquet court, a croquet m-match can sometimes take all day. In fact, I remember one m-m-match that lasted three whole days. The wickets wandered off into the forest and got lost. We had to send the Griffon out to go find them and bring them back. "

The White Rabbit was glassy eyed, and staring off in the distance for a moment until he went on: "The way those wickets are always shuffling here and shuffling there, one would think that they are a deck of playing cards... Oh! Wait a minute..." He slowly exclaimed as if deeply lost in thought. "Now that I think of it, the wickets really *are* a deck of playing cards! Yes! That would explain everything."

Holmes cleared his throat again, raised a pointed finger, and interjected, "Yes that would explain about the croquet match, but I believe you were talking about Alice."

"Oh, yes. Yes, I was. She m-m-missed the following Wednesday as well. And after that, this last Wednesday the M-March Hare was m-missing too. And he has always been there for tea! He m-may be m-m-mad as a M-March Hare and a wee bit hard on the tea service at times, but he has never, ever, ever m-m-missed tea. That is when I went to visit Lewis Carol m-myself, which was no easy task, m-mind you. I was chased by some horrible cats. No offense, Cheshire." He added glancing at the Cheshire Cat, who nodded while sipping his tea, and smiled at the Rabbit. "None taken, Rabbit. Please do go on."

Continuing, his strange tale, he went on, "I had rocks thrown at me by some m-m-monstrous little children, and, when I finally reached Lewis Carroll's front door and knocked, do you know what happened? Do you know what *happened*?"

Sherlock replied rather a-matter-a-factly, "Actually, I wrote a whole series on *The Determination of Impact and Effect of Rocks Thrown Based on Their Starting Location and Trajectory, Divided into Sedimentary, Igneous and Metamorphic Classes of Rocks.* "

With his eyes wide and his ears quivering, the Rabbit paused again and looked around as if frightened. "I'll tell you what happened. When the m-m-maid opened the door, she took one look at me, and screamed! 'Oh no! Not *another* one! Quick, hide the tea service!' and she slammed the door in right my face."

Holmes cocked his head sideways, turned to me and commented, "I can't imagine why she would do that." Turning back to the Rabbit, he asked, "What do you suppose she meant by 'Not *another* one?'"

The White Rabbit, glanced nervously at his watch, before answering, "I am not certain. I can only imagine that perhaps the M-March Hare m-may have been there before m-m-me. You know, he is a bit hard on the tea service. I did not stay to find out. But as I was leaving, I did hear someone inside say if only Mr. Dodgson were still there, he would know what to do about all of the strange creatures showing up at the door, and something about, when is Sherlock Holmes finally going to arrive? Did you tell them you were coming for a visit? It sounded like they were *expecting* you."

Looking rather startled, Holmes shook his head slowly and replied, no, he most certainly had not indicated to anyone at Lewis Carroll's house that he might be going there, and it was rather a surprise to him. Sherlock had been so busy working on an important project over the last three weeks, that he had not spoken to anyone outside of 221-B or even read a newspaper.

The White Rabbit again glanced around nervously, looked down at the floor, and then concluded, "I am afraid that is all I can tell you sir. Alice and the M-March Hare are m-m-missing from Wonderland, and it sounds like Lewis Carol is m-m-missing from here. What are we to do? Can you help us?"

Holmes looked at me and said, "Well, Watson, from what I have just heard, I believe we need to take a trip to visit Charles Dodgson's home in Guildford. I don't think they will slam the door in our face."

Chapter 4. A Very Strange Journey (And somewhat unsettling.)

Of all the journeys that Sherlock Holmes and I had ever taken while working on a case, this was to be one of the strangest. Not only were we going to visit a renowned author, mathematician, and logistician, but we had in tow a semi-intangible talking cat, an overly nervous talking rabbit in a blue waist coat, and a very odd little fellow whose hat was almost as tall as he was.

Now, that would have been strange enough if the three visitors weren't well known characters from a famous children's novel, but they most certainly were three very well known, yet very *imaginary,* literary creations who were sitting right there in Holmes' study, very much alive, drinking his tea, eating his tea cakes, and talking, usually all three of them at the same time. How could that be possible? Before today, if anyone had even suggested the possibility of this, I would have laughed at them, and Sherlock would have dismissed them from the room. Yet, there they all sat. It was very strange indeed.

Utilizing his contacts, and referring to his original copy of *An Alphabetized and Cross-Referenced List of Reliable Carriage Drivers in Greater London,* Holmes was able to hire a trustworthy carriage driver who was willing to drive us the 32 miles to Guildford, as well as to not ask any unnecessary questions about his three unusual passengers. However, the driver did raise his eyebrows considerably as we all climbed aboard, and I do recall him muttering something about, "What does he think this is, Noah's Ark or a circus freak show? But I will say that is a very cute and cuddly rabbit." The White Rabbit cringed noticeably, but wisely did not say a word.

As Sherlock handed the address to the driver with an additional Five Pound note, he thought he glimpsed an unusually large-winged reptilian or bird-like creature lurking in the shadows of a nearby building. He asked me if I had seen it also. I had to confess that I saw nothing in the dense London fog, and when he looked again, it was gone. Sherlock muttered something about wishing he had his *Guide to Unusually Large-Winged Avian Species Native to London and the Surrounding Area* handy.

Sitting down in the coach, he asked our strange guests if perhaps any other Wonderland inhabitants had come to London, at which point they all began gesturing, shaking their heads every which way and answering all at the same time.

"No, no of course not, not at all", Grinned the Cheshire Cat. Adding, "It is not very likely, so I wouldn't think so."

The Hatter held up his head and profoundly announced, "I am not really certain. But then you know I am never really quite certain or sure of anything."

The cat, now squinting as if it were closely examining something slowly added, "Well you know it may just be possible, but I couldn't really tell for sure."

The White Rabbit, with his ears twitching, fearfully murmured, "But it could very well be. One never knows. If that is the case, who could it possibly be?"

And finally, with its eyes opened wide and an even wider grin, the cat proclaimed, "Why now that I think about it, yes, it is entirely possible."

Sherlock looked at me, sighed and commented, "I really must reconsider the way I ask these three a question." Adding under his breath, "Watson, I can see by the morning's proceedings this is going to be a very long and *very* strange day."

Little did he know it would be much longer and far stranger than even he could imagine. The journey began as a fairly normal carriage ride considering the three passengers. The sounds of the street were muted by the wisps of fog that curled and floated through the half light that made up the cold, grey London morning. The clip-clopping of the horse's hooves on the cobblestones seemed to fade into nothingness as the shapeless mist rolled by the coach's window, when suddenly a dark black shadow fell over us, and the coach lurched as if it had been grabbed or snatched from above by something very large and powerful. At the same time, we heard the voice of the coach driver yelling frantically about dragons, demons, never touching whiskey again, and leaving the country. His voice then faded away, as if it was receding far into the distance.

All was silent except for what distinctly sounded like the flapping of a very large set of wings. The motion of the coach became quite smooth and fluid, almost as if we were floating. Not knowing what to expect, I opened the coach window and stuck my head out to see what exactly was going on. What I did see made me quickly pull my head back inside. It was not possible! It could not be! With a look of pure terror on my face, I said to Holmes,

"Sherlock, you are not going to believe this, but I think this coach is airborne, and I feel like I am going to be sick."

Sherlock, sticking his head out the window to assess the situation himself, asked me to pull myself together. Meanwhile, our three visitors started screaming. "It's the Jabberwocky"! The Cheshire Cat wailed.

"Where's the Vorpal Sword?" demanded the Hatter. "We must have the Vorpal Sword!"

"It's too late! We're doomed!" muttered the White Rabbit with his ears twitching wildly.

Knowing Sherlock Holmes as well as I do, and having seen his smooth and confident responses in the most challenging of situations, I can say that it is difficult, if not impossible, to rattle him. However, after pulling his head back into the coach, he certainly appeared more intense and focused than I had ever seen him before. I would even say that he was somewhat unnerved. However with his usual cool and calm demeanor, that is typical of Sherlock Holmes, he addressed me. "Congratulations Watson, I do believe that this time your observations are actually correct. We are most definitely airborne, and the creature that is carrying us is stranger looking than all three of our guests put together. I shall certainly have to write a paper on *The Aerodynamics and Suitability for Air Travel of the Various Types of Cabs and Carriages in Greater London.*"

I began to pull out my service revolver, when Sherlock interrupted me and warned, "We don't dare shoot it, or we'll be in for a long fall back down to the ground."

Turning to the three Wonderland inhabitants, he asked them, "Would any of you happen to know exactly what creature has us in its clutches?" And recalling their usual habit of all talking at once, he added, "Again, if you please, only one at a time."

The Hatter responded by simply pulling his huge hat completely over himself and quivering; the Rabbit with his ears twitching madly, dove under the seat, screaming, "It's too late! We're doomed! We are all doomed"; the cat meanwhile simply vanished into thin air.

"Wonderful!" cried Holmes. "Now what?"

Truthfully, I must confess, I was too overwhelmed to even consider an answer. I had no idea what we were going to do, when we slowly began to experience a gentle downward sensation, followed by the firm but controlled thud of our contact with the ground, and then silence.

I finally managed to pull myself together and ventured, "Why Holmes, I do think we are once again on the ground," and looking out the window I added, "And it looks as if our carriage is parked in the middle of Charles Dodgson's front yard. If this is Lewis Carroll's house, that was the fastest trip from Baker Street to Guildford in history. Although I must say, I wouldn't want to do *that* again."

Holmes, nodding his head in agreement opened the carriage door. "Yes, Watson, that was quite the ride. It was most engaging actually. We are indeed at Dodgson's house, and we seem to have lost our driver and horses somewhere along the way. If we had been set down any closer, we would be inside the house, or at least on top of it. This case is turning out to be most singular and fascinating. I think I would call it 'curious'," he said with a wry grin.

At that point, a local constable came charging through the front gate of the property crying out, "Now see here! You can't park that carriage on a front lawn. Carriages are supposed to stay on the..."

He never did finish his sentence. His jaw dropped, his eyes grew wide, he feebly held up his nightstick in a gesture that was more quivering than threatening, and realizing the absurdity of the situation he dropped the club, turned, and ran back out the gate screaming something about dragons, the gates of hell being unleashed, not ever having signed up for anything at all like this, and moving to France.

As I climbed out of the carriage and looked up at what had caused such fear, I must confess that I almost followed behind him. Sherlock Holmes was completely accurate as always in his assessment that the creature perched on the roof of the coach was most definitely stranger than all three of our visitors put together. In fact, it was stranger than every other bizarre thing I had seen in my entire life combined into one abomination. This was, without question, a creature from one's worst nightmares. I can speak with authority on the subject, having read Sherlock's *A Discussion on the Use of Logic and Laudanum to Analyze and Classify the Intensity and Severity of Nightmares.*

It indeed looked much like a medieval winged dragon or perhaps a giant bat with chicken legs and a long snake-like neck that was as long as its scaly tail. Its claws looked as if they could rip the carriage into splinters without even trying, while its jaws worked like a bear trap. The creature's large eyes were a brilliant bright red, and if its appearance wasn't already strange enough, it was wearing a tweed vest. However, as frightening as it was, it did not appear to be menacing us in any way. It seemed to be preening in a very proud fashion, as if to say, "Wasn't that the fastest carriage ride you have ever had in your whole life? Who needs horses when you have me? We could do it again if you would like. Really we can!"

Sherlock stood his ground before the terrifying creature and boldly addressed it, "Jabberwocky, if you had wanted to kill us you could have easily done so in more than a dozen ways. And I would know, as I wrote a whole series on *The Analysis and Classification of the Number of Ways that Someone Can be Killed in Any Given Situation*, so I deduce that your intentions are not hostile. That, and the fact that you have provided us the fastest journey possible from London to Guilford, although a bit unsettling, tells me that you are as concerned about the current situation as our three guests, *if they would care to come out here*," he added raising the level of his voice so that they could hear him.

Hiding completely under his enormous hat and shaking like a leaf in the wind, the Hatter tiptoed out of the carriage and quickly ran to hide behind a tree, while the White Rabbit took a step outside, looked at the Jabberwocky, and promptly fainted. The Jabberwocky looked at the White Rabbit commenting, "Oh what a cute and cuddly rabbit. Do you think he will be alright?"

The Cheshire Cat, however, materialized his head only on a nearby tree branch and addressed the creature loudly in a rather formal voice: "Jabberwocky! Greetings oh great, manxomeous and winged one! We thank you for the timely transportation. It is most gracious of you."

In a booming, burbling voice the creature replied, "We are all in this together, most nebulous and translucent one. I too am aware of what is happening in Wonderland. The Tweedles, the Door Mouse, and the White Knight have all vanished. Even parts of the royal chess board have started to disappear. Soon there will be nothing left. I see that none of you are brandishing a Vorpal Sword, so I felt safe in providing assistance with the transportation aspect of this adventure. Time *is* of the essence, and nothing can compare to air travel."

Gesturing with one of his long claws in the direction of Sherlock, the creature pointed out, "You are very wise in seeking the assistance of this logical and deductive one. I can tell by his demeanor that he sees a great deal more than most anyone else. Looking into his eyes, it is obvious that he understands the meaning of what he sees more clearly than everyone else."

The Jabberwocky, twisting his snake like neck so that his head faced in front of Sherlock and looking straight into his eyes, went on, "I see too that he unquestionably deduces the implications of what he sees and the significance of what he understands more completely than anyone I have ever met. I believe he would make a really great detective. I am talking 'world class' here. He could become truly legendary. I imagine they will write volumes of books about him if he doesn't plunge to his death over a waterfall or something like that. I shall like to engage him in a game of chess, should we bring this conundrum to a positive conclusion. In the mean time, let us not lose our heads over it all."

Sherlock, meanwhile, had casually taken his clay pipe out of his jacket pocket and was filling it with tobacco as he carefully studied the beast and listened to its conversation with the Cheshire Cat. The Jabberwocky pointed a long claw at the pipe and in an equally casual voice, commented, "I *can* light that pipe for you, oh deep and contemplative one, but you would probably want to stand several feet away from it while I do. You may want to keep a bucket of water on hand as well, but I would still recommend staying away from waterfalls. They can be dangerous, you know."

Sherlock hastily returned his pipe to his jacket pocket and replied, "Ah, no thank you, most scaly and undulating one. That's quite all right. Perhaps now is not the best time for a pipe. But if you can explain your presence here and that most exhilarating ride, it would be much appreciated."

The Jabberwocky peered directly at Sherlock and started to explain that not only were the inhabitants of Wonderland starting to vanish, but parts of Wonderland itself were disappearing along with the boundaries between London and Wonderland. Just the other day, as he flew above the Tulgey Woods, he thought he had seen, sticking up through the clouds, a large tower with clocks on it. I knew he must have been referring to Big Ben and wondered what was going to happen next.

Before the creature could go on, however, the front door of Charles Dodgson's house slowly creaked open and a white haired butler wearing a black suit and waving an envelope in his hand stepped out nervously and announced, "Well, it's about time you arrived, Mr. Sherlock Holmes." Looking towards the White Rabbit, he added, "My goodness this certainly is a cute and cuddly rabbit you have here." Returning his gaze to Sherlock, he went on. "I was not sure whether our chinaware could hold out much longer. I am James, the butler, and I have a letter for you from the late Charles Lutwidge Dodgson, who passed away just three weeks ago. I have instructions to invite you in for tea, with what little tea service is left. However, you, fine and scaly sir," and he pointed at the Jabberwocky, "will have to sit on the front porch and perhaps stick your head through the window into the tea room, if that is acceptable. And as we do not have any tea cups suitable for something of your size, would a large beer stein work for you as a tea cup?"

The Jabberwocky's eyes lit up considerably and he responded that the arrangements were quite satisfactory as long as the tea was Earl Grey and that there was plenty of cream. He cheerfully volunteered to quickly fetch a cow if necessary, to which the butler assured him that it, was not.

Holmes looked at me as if deep in thought and commented, "This sadly answers the question regarding the whereabouts of Lewis Carroll. I have been so involved in that project these last three weeks that I never saw the news of his death in the papers. This is still a most curious and unusual case, Watson. I am sure it will be one for your journals, although I seriously doubt anyone would believe it. You may consider postponing its publication for quite some time if you value your reputation as an author or continued future as a practicing doctor. Shall we go inside and have some tea and see what the late Charles Dodgson had to say to me? The presence of that letter tells me that he had some idea of what exactly is going on here, and we may receive more answers. Also, if you could rouse the rabbit and extract Mr. Hatter from his hiding place, that would be excellent."

Chapter 5. Another Very Strange Tea Party (I guess it can get more unusual.)

A multitude of wild thoughts and questions ran through my mind as we entered the house of the late Lewis Carroll. How could he have possibly known three weeks in advance that Sherlock Holmes would be calling for him? What was in the letter, and how would it affect the outcome of all this? How was it possible that the imaginary characters from his books had actually come to life, and what was happening to them now that he had recently passed away? What must be going through the ever-so-logical-and-practical-mind of Sherlock Holmes as all of this unfolded? And finally, where in the world would this incredibly strange adventure lead us to next?

The answer to my last question was quickly forthcoming, as we were directed into the tea room, where a table with scones, tea sandwiches, tea cakes, and other savories, along with several pots of tea, a mismatched set of chipped tea cups, and one large beer stein were waiting for us.

Entering the tea room, I noticed that the Jabberwocky had already curled itself up on the front porch outside the window, with its long scaly neck and arms extending into the room. It was resting its head on the back of one of the stuffed chairs and addressing the butler. "You know, if you need help preparing more tea sandwiches, I could fetch a lamb or a goat and roast it in a jiffy," The Jabberwocky was telling the butler, while the butler did his very best to assure the creature that it would not be necessary. The Jabberwocky replied, "Suit yourself, oh ancient and laboring one."

Emptying an entire tray of tea sandwiches at once into its wide open jaws, he handed the empty tray back to the butler commenting, "Hmm, pickled herring! Those are some of my favorites. Might you have any more of them? Oh, and I will take that stein of tea now, if you please; Earl Grey, if you have it."

The Cheshire Cat with its typical wide grin was casually enjoying its cup of tea with milk, while the White Rabbit appeared to be trying to hide behind his tea cup with very little success, finally abandoning the tea cup for a somewhat larger tea pot. The Hatter was no longer hiding inside his enormous top hat but instead was devouring tea cakes from a three-tiered tray.

As Holmes and I settled into our own tea and scones, the butler cleared his throat and made an announcement: "My dear guests" -- And I did notice a slight hesitation at the word 'guests'-- "The night that Rev. Charles Lutwidge Dodgson, better known as Lewis Carroll passed away, he gave me this letter with instructions that it should be delivered into the hand of a Mr. Sherlock Holmes when he arrived here, of which the Master assured me that Mr. Holmes eventually would. The Master did mention that we might first experience a few 'odd' visitors prior to the arrival of Mr. Holmes, which we also have. He did not, however, mention exactly how odd the visitors might be or that we would experience a significant decrease in the amount of usable chinaware as a result of any such odd visitors."

At that point, the White Rabbit straightened up and

exclaimed, "Then the M-M-March Hare was here before I arrived! That explains a part of it, or at least the condition of the china." Looking nervously in the direction of the Butler, the White Rabbit slouched down and resumed trying to hide behind a tea pot.

The butler looked downward at the White Rabbit and muttered, "Indeed!" Looking directly at Sherlock Holmes, he went on, "The Master seemed to feel that after you read the letter and figure out exactly what to do, the problem will be solved and all will once again be back to normal. However, I am not certain that 'normal' will ever be truly normal again. He instructed me to invite you and who or whatever is with you in for tea."

Pausing and looking around the room with a skeptical gaze, he continued, "Here is your letter. Tea has been served. I will leave you to your discussions. Please ring if you need more tea or sandwiches."

At that point, the Jabberwocky waved another empty sandwich tray in one claw while vigorously ringing the bell rope with the other. The butler retrieved the tray and exited the room muttering something about certainly checking to make sure his next position was not working for an author, while consoling himself that at least he had not worked for Mary Shelley or Bram Stoker.

As the door closed behind the butler, Sherlock Holmes gingerly held up and examined the letter from the late Lewis Carroll. The envelope was pale lilac in color and of a heavy stock with a dark wax seal upon it as if it contained news of impending doom. He looked from the envelope and stated, "Did you know Watson, that last year I wrote a paper on *The Identification of Stationary*

31

Manufacturers Throughout Western Europe Based on Color, Texture and Weight of Envelopes? I can tell you who manufactured this envelope, where it was made, what day of the week it was produced, and whether the machine operator was right handed or left handed."

I replied that none of that was really important and asked why he doesn't just read the letter as this case was getting stranger by the minute. Sherlock conjectured that he didn't think it could possibly get any stranger than it already was, and he proceeded to tear open the letter and read it.

As he read the letter out loud, I realized that, contrary to Holmes' comment, it was indeed getting much stranger than either of us could have ever possibly imagined.

Chapter 6. A Very Strange Letter (And rather cryptic at that.)

"My Dear Mr. Holmes (and you too, Dr. Watson) as well as any of my dear and wonderfully strange creations who might still be there with you:

"I offer you this letter as a last resort to help preserve my legacy and the lives of all those whom I have brought into being through the writing of Alice's Adventures in Wonderland.

"If there is anyone who can work though the strange logic and cryptic nature of this situation, it is you Mr. Holmes. For without question, next to me, you are the most logically-minded person in the world. I have read your landmark monograph on *The Value of Observation, Deduction and Logic in Determining Hidden but True Facts Versus Obvious but False Facts.* Yet I assure you, that to solve this puzzle, you will have to call upon the very illogical creatures whose existence must seem so unlikely and improbable to you. You truly must embrace the reality of them in order to succeed."

At that point, Holmes had to temporarily interrupt his reading of the letter to deal with a strong hug from the Hatter and the nuzzling from the head of the Jabberwocky while at the same time trying to reason with them, and extricate himself from the Cheshire Cat's tail which was wrapped around his neck, as the cat had apparently materialized on top of Sherlock's head.

"All of you please contain yourselves!" He exclaimed. "If any of you were really listening, he asked me to embrace your *'reality*,' not all of you physically! You must trust me. As odd and unusual as this is, I accepted the reality of this highly illogical and most improbable situation exactly two hours and twenty three minutes ago. The sooner we complete this puzzling, paradoxical prospect, the sooner we can, all of us, return to some semblance of normality, or whatever it is that stands for normal where you come from. Now let us continue reading the letter."

Nodding affirmatively, the Jabberwocky withdrew his head and voiced his agreement. "Yes indeed, most logical and far seeing one. We must continue the reading of the letter. This is quite wise as one would expect from someone as analytical and rational as yourself, even if you don't appreciate a fond, friendly embrace."

The Hatter returned to his tea cakes while the Cheshire Cat mostly dematerialized leaving only a wide smile looking rather like a glowing halo above Sherlock's head as he went on reading the letter.

"My story begins like so many often do, at the very beginning. But the question is: Where is that beginning? The answer is that it has been lost, and you must find it. You must return to the exact moment that Wonderland came to life, so to speak; for it is there that you will be able to correct the problem at hand. Time is running out!

"I must stress that time is of the essence, but not time as you know it. Most people look at time as a river flowing in one direction in which we are all swept along with no control whatsoever over our direction or destination. But you must believe me, this is false. I have discovered it is possible to step out of the river of time on to the shore of a reality that is outside of the boundaries of time. One can walk upon that shore in both directions, forward or backward, and then step back into the river at any point of their choosing. I have done, it Mr. Holmes, and I assure you that you can do it as well. And you must do so in order to set right what has gone so terribly wrong."

The serious tone of the letter caused the Hatter to lose interest in his tea cakes, while the White Rabbit stared at his watch so intently I thought he was going to burn a hole into it. The Cheshire Cat's smile meanwhile, had vanished from above Sherlock's head. The entire cat reappeared sitting upright upon the fireplace mantel with its tail hanging downward and swishing back and forth like the pendulum of a clock his eyes looking back and forth to the right and left in coordination with his swishing tail. It felt as if, with each second that passed, we were coming closer to a horrible conclusion.

Continuing the letter, Holmes read on, "While it is possible to step out of the river of time, it is not without its complications or ramifications. There are Time Guardians who closely control the manipulation of time, and they are the most logical of creatures in existence. Any time one steps out of the river, the Time Guardians are watching and waiting, ready to pose logic puzzles to any who dare choose that path. And with each additional instance a person attempts time travel, the Guardians create more complex and convoluted logic puzzles.

"When I first stepped out of the river of time many years ago, their logic puzzles were mere child's play to someone of my skills in logic. I felt so confident in my ability to solve any logic puzzle they could come up with, that I convinced them to agree to a wager. To me, the risk was more than worth the gain. What I gained in the wager with them, was life for Alice and all of the creatures of Wonderland, as well as Wonderland itself. What I risked was the loss of Wonderland and everyone in it if the Guardian's final logic puzzle could not be solved in the time period provided. I was certain that I had all the time in the world required for solving their final enigma of logic, for like you, Sherlock, I am a master of logic and deduction. However, the one thing I could not predict was the failure of my health. I am dying, but Wonderland and all of its marvelous and most unusual beings must not die with me. With each passing day, the borders that contain Wonderland grow weaker, and more and more of its inhabitants will find their way to earth and whatever awaits them here, or they will just plain disappear.

"You must figure out how to step outside of time and then solve the final logic puzzle before February 5. Per the rules set forth by the Time Guardians, I myself cannot tell you how to step out of the river of time, but I assure you, there are horrendously great wells of possible ways to do so, and each one is unique to the individual. Once you have done so, it is then that you must solve the world's greatest logic puzzle, and Wonderland, with all of my most illogical of creations, will survive.

Sincerely yours,
Charles Lutwidge Dodgson, or to my friends, and I do count you as a friend, Lewis Carroll"

Chapter 7. A Very Strange Discussion (Well, it's about time.)

In the profound silence that followed, I noticed several things: The White Rabbit was staring out the window in a daze, not even noticing that his pocket watch was immersed in his cup of tea, and the Hatter was sniffling and blowing his nose using the window curtains as a handkerchief as he moaned, "That was the most touching, saddest letter I have ever heard someone read." To which the Cheshire Cat responded, "Hatter, you know very well that that is the only letter you have ever heard someone read. I am not saying that you are not well read; in fact, your nose is quite red at the moment. Why it is almost bright red enough to read by. But I will agree that it was quite touching and more than a bit sad. Would you care to use the table cloth as well?" The Cat then proceeded to yank the entire table cloth off the table without upsetting a single thing upon it. He handed it to the Hatter who promptly used it to blow his nose, which sounded something like a donkey with a sore throat braying through an out of tune trombone.

The Jabberwocky, meanwhile, was contemplating his empty tea stein, woefully wondering how much time, if any, was left and whether or not there was enough time for more tea sandwiches. Deciding there was, indeed, enough time, he began vigorously pulling on the bell rope -- unfortunately pulling it right off the ceiling -- and then wondering out loud, "Now how are we to get refills?"

I myself was wondering what on earth we were going to do next. I had not seen any clues in the letter about how to step out of the 'river of time', as he called it. He had made it very clear *what* to do, but with no real instructions about *how* to go about doing it. We were no better off than before we arrived. I voiced my thoughts to Sherlock who had remained in a contemplative silence since he finished reading the letter. In his usual form, he immediately admonished me for my lack of vision and understanding.

"Oh Watson, my dear short-sighted friend, have you learned nothing at all from our many adventures together? Have you not read my report, *On Listening to What Has Not Been Said to Determine What Has Actually Been Said in Any Given Statement?* Did you not listen to the letter I just read? Were you not paying attention? In any logic puzzle, there are rules, spoken and unspoken. Some things must be inferred, while others are clearly given. Some clues are revealed, while others are hidden. One must analytically examine the information provided to reveal the answer. In any collection of information, there is the obvious background material, and there are the less than obvious real facts hidden between the lines. The ultimate logic puzzle itself will only be given to me when I reach the reality outside of time."

"But how are we to do that?" I exclaimed. "Dodgson said there are many possible ways to do it, but he did not mention a single one of them. He did not even provide any clues! We are no better off now than we were before we arrived."

"Ah, but he did Watson, old boy; he most certainly did. Think back for a moment. He did not say there are many possible ways. What he was *most* specific to say is that 'There are horrendously great wells of possible ways'. Do you not see it, Watson? 'Horrendously Great Wells', *H. G.*

Wells! He is the author who recently wrote a novel about time travel. 'The Time Machine', I think it was called. It must be Wells that Dodgson is referring to. He will be our next destination in this most curious and strange adventure. We must go see him immediately."

I was thunderstruck! I could not believe what I was hearing. "Holmes!" I cried, "What *are* you thinking? Have you completely lost your sense of logic and reason? How can you even suggest that we go chasing after the author of some fictional story about time travel? He is not a physicist or even a scientist. All he did is write a fictional novel about a completely imaginary machine that somehow travels through time. How is that supposed to help us?"

Holmes spread his arm in a wide circle as if to encompass all of the creatures in the room and answered me, "Look around you, Watson. We are surrounded by completely imaginary creatures that somehow really do exist and are right here in this room with us. How do you explain that? You and I saw with our own eyes as the Cheshire Cat walked through a solid wooden door and left real cat hair on my pants leg .I examined the cat hair and verified it was real."

The Cheshire Cat, interrupted licking his paw, and grinned, "I may be able to pass through solid wooden doors and vanish at will, but I am still a cat. What can I say? Like it or not, cat hair goes with the territory, so to speak."

Sherlock ignored the Cheshire and continued, "The Hatter and the White Rabbit drank our tea and ate our teacakes. The tea and cakes had to go somewhere. They didn't just magically disappear from the table. You know there is no such thing as magic, but as strange as all of this seems, what we have been experiencing here is real. Of course I shall have to rewrite my paper on *The Examination, Determination and Validation of Reality From Multiple Visual Perspectives, With an Emphasis on the Unreal.*"

Pointing towards the Jabberwocky, who cheerfully waved an empty sandwich tray back at him, he asked, "And him? How would you explain him and the near instantaneous ride from London to Guildford? Watson, we are in entirely new territory here. The old laws of reality and logic simply do not apply in this adventure."

At that point, we were interrupted by a timid knock on the tea room door as the butler opened it bringing in more refreshments and saying, "Excuse me sirs, but there is a Unicorn here demanding to see you. He insists that it is most urgent."

A *Unicorn*? This was the final straw. I threw up my hands in surrender and told the butler to send him in, but the Unicorn had apparently not waited for a formal invitation into the room and came trotting in past the butler, nearly knocking the food tray from his hands, and commenting as he went by, "I do hope there is some plum cake on that tray or at least some good brown bread."

I could not believe my eyes! A Unicorn had just walked into the room like it had belonged there. Imaginary or not, the creature was truly magnificent! One could not help but be in awe of its majesty. Its coat was whiter than the proverbial newly fallen snow, or for that matter anything else one could think of to compare it to. It was as if the

Unicorn was the very definition of the color white, and every other thing that aspired to be that color was just a pale imitation.

Looking towards Sherlock Holmes, the Unicorn pointed his beautiful spiral horn directly at him and spoke: "You must forgive your friend, Mr. Holmes. All the years of working with you and recording your unerring logic and deduction functioning like clockwork has jaded his point of view. He still does not understand that true logic looks at every possibility, even the impossible or illogical ones."

Turning to look at me, the Unicorn rested its glowing horn upon my shoulder and in a timeless voice said to me, *"Believe,* Watson. Just *believe.* I really am a Unicorn. I really am standing right here in front of you. Your friend Sherlock Holmes is truly headed in the right direction. He is on the path to his destiny."

The peace, warmth and for lack of a better word 'light' I felt flowing through my entire body on that day was so beautiful and utterly beyond description, I know I shall treasure and remember it always…

However, the wonder of the moment was particularly short lived, as the Unicorn then quickly emptied the nearest three cups of tea and stated to no one in particular, "Now, can we can have some of that plum cake before we leave for Mr. Wells' home? My long-time sparring partner, the Lion, has already vanished, and I really do not want to be the next one to disappear."

Turning back towards Sherlock, he pointed out: "You are absolutely correct, Mr. Holmes. We must quickly go to the house of H. G. Wells. He published his work, 'The Time

Machine' as a fictional novel, but I tell you he really has created a device for traveling through time. With all due modesty, Unicorns are faster, more nebulous and much more transitory than even Cheshire Cats. No offense Cheshire." To which the Cheshire Cat simply grinned and winked. "And I have been to the house of H. G. Wells, and seen his Time Machine for myself. This is indeed the next truly logical step in this journey."

Holmes simply nodded in agreement and smiled as he put his arm around my shoulder saying, "So you see, Watson? You have a real live Unicorn telling you that a visit to the time travel author is the next *logical* step. What more proof could you want?"

What could I possibly say to him? I broke down and agreed that we should go to Wells' home. Then the White Rabbit, roused from its deep concentration, waved its pocket watch in the air and voiced its approval adding, "So it *is* about time. I suspected that all along. I just hope we are not too late."

The Hatter giggled and replied, "You all know that I am never really quite certain or sure of anything, but I would almost feel relatively safe to say that between having the undisputed master of logic and deduction, a Jabberwocky that can fly a coach from London to Guildford in record time, and a real live Unicorn, we stand a fair to moderate chance of not being too late. In fact we *may* even be on time, but don't quote me on that. If you do insist on quoting someone, quote the White Rabbit. You can tell him, that I said it is perfectly fine with me."

The Cheshire Cat rematerialized on the brim of the Hatters top hat swishing its tail in the Hatter's face mewing, "Don't forget about me, Hatter. I was the one that found Sherlock Holmes and convinced him to help us. Nothing gets one's attention like phasing through a solid wooden door. Of course some well placed cat hair always helps. I am quite good at that also."

Sherlock interrupted and pointed out that Lewis Carroll had clearly stated that we were all equally important in this endeavor; however, if we really didn't want to end up being too late, then we had better leave soon, at which point, the tea party adjourned, and we headed back to the coach.

Chapter 8. Another Very Strange Journey (And this time quite a bit more unsettling.)

As we exited the house of the late Lewis Carroll, we thanked the butler for his hospitality and the lovely refreshments. We tried to apologize for the condition of the bell rope, curtains, and table cloth. But he said not to worry, everything was just fine, and do come back soon, any time, but please check first as he may be leaving town in the near future. In fact, he may be leaving the country in the near future. As I recall, he said something about going to somewhere far away from libraries and authors.

I noticed that when we did finally leave, he was in a heated discussion with a bed of talking flowers that had suddenly appeared on the front porch and were trying to find a way into the house. I recall him saying something about never, in all his years as a gentleman's butler, had he ever had to try and reason with roses, bicker with begonias, or debate with daisies, and what *was* this world coming to when a butler had to be zoo keeper, a gardener, and serve tea to a dragon, (I am assuming he meant the Jabberwocky), all in the same afternoon.

In order to get back to London as soon as possible, we agreed that the Jabberwocky would again carry the coach with us all except the Unicorn, who knew the way to Wells' house and would guide the Jabberwocky from the ground. We did have to break up a minor disagreement about who was actually faster, with Jabberwocky saying that Unicorns were no faster than drying paint, while the Unicorn commented that he had already been there and back again three times in the time it took the Jabberwocky to finish its sentence.

Sherlock pointed out that if they wanted to be precise on the subject they could consult his report on *The Speed of Drying Paint in Varying Temperature and Humidity Conditions with an Emphasis on the Viscosity of the Paint;* however, they had better come to some sort of an agreement very quickly, or it would not matter who was the fastest, because they would both disappear quicker than he could say, "On your mark, get set, go!" That did get their attention.

Once again, the carriage flew through the dreary fog-bound skies of London in the claws of the Jabberwocky; however, instead of a relatively smooth Point-A-to-Point-B, straight-as-the-crow-flies (or in this case straight-as-the-Jabberwocky-flies) type of flight path as we had previously taken on the way to Guilford, we were subjected to a flight path that closely resembled a Tasmanian Devil let loose in a labyrinth.

While the Unicorn was incredibly swift, indeed faster than the wind, unfortunately, it did need to follow the surface roads and streets, which it accomplished at speeds far beyond anyone's imagination. The creature was capable of turning 90-degree corners, of which there were a great many, in a quarter second or less and then taking off again at speeds even faster than it had approached the corners. It would not have been so bad had the Jabberwocky not tried to follow the *very same exact path* as the Unicorn. Needless to say, being in the coach, we felt as if we were inside of a box tied to the back of a mad bull with firecrackers attached to its tail as it crossed the English Channel in a small craft during a full gale.

In the split second that we took off, covering three miles and navigating the first eighteen corners almost instantaneously, several things inside the coach happened at once. The Cat vanished into thin air, the Hatter seemed to fold himself up into his hat, which was bouncing off the walls of the coach, and the White Rabbit leaped into my arms crying, "Save me! Save me!"

Sherlock and I held on to the coach for dear life, as the coach did its best to hold on to itself for dear life and remain intact despite the wild ride. It almost succeeded in doing so, but if you recall the newspapers of the next day, February 5, 1898, there was a brief article about it raining wagon wheels from the sky in various parts of London. Authorities were most perplexed, and Sherlock made a note to provide extra compensation to the coach driver should he ever turn up.

As one would imagine, we did get to H. G. Wells' house in record time. Of course, it was minus the coach's wheels and various other odd parts, I am sure. As we stepped out of what little remained of the carriage, the Unicorn was casually waiting next to the front steps of the house, inquiring, "What took you so long?" to which the Jabberwocky responded, "We could have made it in half the time had you not taken the scenic route."

While I myself thankfully and unsteadily set my feet back on solid ground, the White Rabbit leaped from my arms to the ground kissing it and crying, never again would it even think of air travel. The Hatter extracted himself from his battered and bruised hat and crawled to the ground with a huge sigh of relief and a groan. Meanwhile, in his usual indefatigable and stoic manner,

Holmes merely brushed off his sleeves saying, "You know, Watson, once the kinks are worked out of it, I do believe that there is a solid future in travel by air. Yes, a really solid future." At that point, the Jabberwocky released its grip on the coach which completely collapsed into a pile of wood and leather. Looking back at the pile of debris, Sherlock added, "Like I said, it does need to have a few details worked out." Then as an afterthought, he added, "Watson, do remember to remind me to make arrangements for a replacement coach for our driver whenever we find him. I believe this carriage has definitely reached the end of its useful life."

The Cheshire Cat, with its eyes looking a tad greener than usual, but with its characteristically wide grin unfazed, faded back into solid form sitting on top of the remains of the coach, and stated, "I say, fellow sky travelers, once we resolve the current uncertainty at hand, we should start a sky tour company. I can see it now! *See all of London in less than a minute! (Having lunch or dinner beforehand definitely not recommended. Not for the squeamish or faint of heart.) This is a once-in-a-life-time experience!*"

"That is because once anyone has done it, they would never ever want to do it again," groaned The Hatter. "Not to mention you would need to replace the coach after every flight!"

"Well, yes, you may have something there," acknowledged the Cat as it surveyed the ruins of the coach.

The door to the home opened and out stepped H. G. Wells himself. Surveying the odd group of travelers and the remains of the demolished coach in his front yard, he smiled and said, "Do come in. I have been expecting you."

Chapter 9. A Very Strange Meeting (Maybe H. G. Wells does have the answer.)

In response to the invitation to enter the house, the Jabberwocky raised a claw and posed a question: "Greetings, oh chronologically gifted one. I was wondering whether or not that invitation included me. You do understand, considering my size and all, I would be quite happy to rest out here on the porch as long there is an open window in close proximity to the gathering room and reasonable access to refreshments."

Wells replied that either way was fine, as both the doors and the sitting room were large enough to accommodate all of them. The Jabberwocky burbled his enthusiasm and galumphed up the stairs, into the house, and directly into the sitting room finding an open place in a corner not far from the refreshment table sighing, "Ah, Earl Grey, and pickled herring sandwiches, my two favorites." The rest of us followed him into the room and found seats, except for the Unicorn, who chose to remain standing on the other side of the refreshment table closer to the tea.

Wells entered and began with the question, "Would anyone care for tea and refreshments?" To which everyone but Holmes, the Unicorn, and the Jabberwocky cried out in unison, "No thank you! Not just yet if you don't mind," with the White Rabbit adding, "Please! Can we first let the ground stop spinning?"

Wells again nodded affirmatively and smiled, giving me the opportunity to observe him. H. G. Wells at the time was 32 years of age, of medium build, with dark hair and a drooping mustache. He had been a struggling writer for some time, and the sudden success of his novel, The Time Machine, three years before had set quite well with him with several more literary successes following since then. With a soft smile he addressed the group.

"Gentleman and visitors from Wonderland, your reputations precede you, and I am honored to be in your company. Mr. Holmes, your fame as the world's foremost consulting detective and master of logic and deduction is without equal. When I heard of the passing of Lewis Carroll, I knew it would not be long before you would be calling on me. That and several sightings of a Unicorn in the vicinity of my house told me that you would soon be here to discuss the possibilities of time travel. Am I not correct, Mr. Holmes?"

Sherlock nodded and agreed with him adding, "Indeed, Mr. Wells. We are here to talk about time travel and logic puzzles. I can see by the flower in your lapel that you are experienced in time travel, as that particular botanical specimen is not to be found In London at this time of year, or for that matter, anywhere else on the planet in this particular time period. I shall have to add it to my *Guide to Identifying Flowers Originating Outside of this Reality*. Recalling my paper on *The Analysis, Identification, Verification and Determination of the Origin of all Soils to be Found in London, England* and looking at the soil residue on your shoes tells me that it did not come from anywhere in London. I can also see that a large device was recently dragged from your garden into what I presume is your laboratory. I won't bore you with the details from my *Analysis of Drag Marks Based on a Scientific Study of 11,373 Objects Categorized by Size, Shape and Density*. Also your complexion tells me that you have recently been in sunnier climates than London in the middle of winter."

I then jokingly added, "Or sunnier than London most any time of year, for that matter. I don't need a technical paper to tell me that. One hardly ever sees the sun any more it's been so foggy these last few years."

Wells responded affirmatively, "Yes to both of you. The soil residue and flower you speak of, Mr. Homes, are not at all from this time period, and Dr. Watson you would be amazed at the climates I have experienced up until recently."

The Hatter taking the pose of a public speaker offered, "As uncertain as I most always find myself, I am quite sure it was sunny the last time I was in Wonderland. But who knows if the sun is still there. If the sun is gone, that means there are no more Sundays. Can you imagine *two* Mondays in a row?"

The Unicorn then commented, "It was still there when I left yesterday, and the letter stated that Mr. Holmes had until February 5 to complete the logic puzzle. But if that is the case, then why are the inhabitants of Wonderland already vanishing?"

"That is because the time frame to complete the logic puzzle is nearing its completion," stated Wells. "The framework that holds Wonderland together is weakening and the boundaries are failing. Once the puzzle is solved, I am certain that Wonderland will return to its original state with all of its inhabitants, but I am getting ahead of myself."

The Cheshire Cat, now just a floating head with a wide

grin, then interjected, "Well, that would give you a healthy "head" start in any kind of a race, wouldn't it? You could even "head" them off at the pass so to speak."

Holmes responded by pointing out to the Cat, "Cheshire, I really do accept your presence here, as highly improbable as it may be. However, that does not mean I have to accept your completely illogical musings."

Rotating his head completely upside down, the cat replied, "Would you prefer illogical mewing? As a cat, I am entitled to mew all I care to, logical or illogical." Cheshire started mewing both forward and backwards as well as upside down until Sherlock stepped directly in front of it, cleared his throat loudly and asked me if I happened to have my service revolver handy. The Cat then immediately ceased its mewing and vanished leaving a tail waving a white flag.

Sherlock then turned to Wells, and said, "Please do continue and hopefully without any more nonsensical interruptions."

Wells began his story in earnest. "My personal experience in time travel began several years ago. It was while I wrote my novel, The Time Machine, which as I am sure the Unicorn has told you, is based mostly on fact. Although I was able to successfully build a time travel device, I knew I could never let the public or the government know that such a device really exists. So I wrote my story as a fictional novel. Society has made such a complete mess of things on their own; I shudder to think what they would do with the power the Time Machine could provide. I created the device because I thought I could find a different time period where my views were more common and the society that lived by such views would be perfect, but alas, I discovered that no such time frame exists.

"Returning to time travel itself: While I focused on a mechanical-crystal-driven approach, in my brief acquaintance with Lewis Carroll, I discovered that he had utilized an optical-mirror-based approach to time travel. He briefly alluded to that in a roundabout way in his story, *Alice's Adventure Through the Looking Glass*. By the way, Mr. Holmes, I did read your article on *The Optical and Refractive Properties of Looking Glasses Based on Temperature of Formation with an Emphasis on Polishing Compounds Used*. That was quite interesting, and I was not aware of the significant difference between polishing a mirror clockwise and counter-clockwise.

Wells resumed his explanation: "Each person's approach to time travel is unique and individual, suited to their own abilities and inclinations. I am sure that yours would be logic based, Mr. Holmes. The secret is to truly believe, with every fiber of your being, that you *can* step out of the river of time and create the methodology or mechanical construct required to make it happen. It is entirely up to you how you do it. Once you achieve success, it is then that you will meet the Time Guardians.

"As time is a logical progression of events, the Guardians are the most logical beings. While some randomness in time is normal and to be expected, the Guardians exist for the purpose of maintaining order in the flow of time. Whenever someone randomly steps out of the river to time travel, that person must answer a logic riddle or puzzle to be able to continue. The more one time travels, the more challenging the puzzle becomes. If one cannot solve the

Guardian's puzzle, they will be returned to their own time period, never to time travel again."

Wells paused for a moment with a look of sadness before he regained his focus. "I myself am now finished with time traveling. The logic puzzles have reached a level far beyond my capabilities, so sadly my device no longer functions for me. Lewis Carroll was a master of logic. He was so certain that he could solve their ultimate logic enigma, that he not only risked his continued ability to time travel, but the lives of all of Wonderland as well. The arrangement he made with them was to bring Wonderland into existence and give life to all its inhabitants, but if the ultimate logic puzzle was not solved by the fifth of this month, which is tomorrow, then Wonderland with all of its inhabitants, will vanish forever."

"Tomorrow?" the White Rabbit loudly exclaimed. "Did you say we are all going to vanish TOMORROW? We're all doomed! It's too late! I knew it. I knew we would be too late." The White Rabbit sadly placed his gold watch back in his pocket, slumped down in his chair and slid to the floor ending up under the table as Wells resumed.

"It *may* not be too late, my friends. You see the importance of your presence here, Mr. Holmes. You must go against the very foundation of your logic and reason to embrace the reality of all of this, as impossible as it all seems," he made a wide sweep of his hand, "in order to call upon that very same logic to solve the world's greatest logic puzzle. It is indeed a conundrum."

The room was utterly silent as Wells completed his story, poured a cup of tea for himself, and sat down in one of the chairs.

Sherlock Holmes sat as if in a trance for the second time that day. Once again, I could almost see the gears of logic, reason, and deduction turning inside his brain. I myself still saw nothing that he could do to resolve the situation. I did raise the question if it were possible for another person to use Wells' time machine, someone other than himself, who was not yet bound by the restrictive rules of the Guardians.

"That is an excellent question, Dr. Watson," he replied. "But who would be willing to risk using the creation of another person's mind to travel to an ethereal-other-worldly place that, in all practicality, logically does not even exist? My mind, intellect, reasoning, and thinking process are an integral part of the functionality of that Time Machine. How would another person's thinking and reality interact and function with it? There's really no telling what would happen. They might get permanently lost in time or possibly even end up on the planet Mars! Who knows? I have no idea if it would even function for someone else."

At that very moment, the whole room started to tremble and shudder slightly, and the lights began to flicker. We all looked around at each other wondering what was going on when H.G. Wells' eyes grew wide in shock and fear as he exclaimed, "My Time Machine! Someone is in the laboratory using my Time Machine!"

In a panic, we raced down the hallway to his laboratory to see the White Rabbit his ears twitching wildly, sitting in the velvet passenger seat of a beautiful brass and varnished wood sled-like device with a large spinning disc on the back of it and a series of blinking lights on the control console in front of the seat. The rabbit's paws were firmly clutching the crystal control lever.

"No!" cried out Wells, "It's too dangerous!"

"But we are out of time!" screamed the White Rabbit as he frantically pulled down on the crystal control lever.

"Somebody stop him!", exclaimed Wells.

As the machine began to blur growing more intangible by the second, Holmes, the Hatter, the Cheshire Cat, the Unicorn, the Jabberwocky, and myself all made a frantic leap for the machine to try to stop the Rabbit. We all made contact with the Time Machine, but it was too late. In a blinding flash of light, everything seemed to blur and the room disappeared completely.

Chapter 10. A Very Strange Side Trip (Who would have ever imagined this?)

We clung frantically to the Time Machine as it whirled through space and time taking us to who knows where. This time I had to agree with the White Rabbit and felt that we were all doomed. I was sure there would be no return from this journey. An unending array of lights and scenes raced past us in a multicolored kaleidoscope of blurry images. As we rushed past the moon, it seemed as if I could have reached down and touched it. I had never in my life seen the stars so huge and bright. A comet with a glittering tail of ice crystals and glowing dust particles streaked by so close I thought it would hit us. Where was this infernal machine taking us to?

I looked down towards the control console and saw Sherlock reaching desperately for the crystal lever. He was trying to maintain his grip on the machine and, at the same time, gain control of the device. At last he was able to get his hands on it and gradually pull the lever back to the stop position. The sounds and lights had ceased as the spinning disc gradually had come to rest and we finally stopped. But where in creation were we?

"Where *are* we?" queried the Hatter? "This time, I really am sure this is not Wonderland or Londonland or any other land that I can recall visiting. And I am typically never really quite certain or sure of anything."

The Cheshire Cat piped in: "That's because you have never been to anywhere other than Wonderland or Londonland, as you call it. Unless you want to count the visit to Lewis Carroll's house in Guildford as a separate land since we did actually 'land' there after our carriage flight. That was a quite an *uplifting* experience. It's too bad the carriage did not survive. Once this adventure is brought to a successful conclusion, if I want to travel by air again, I guess I will have to just *'wing it.'* Ha! 'Wing it' get it?"

Ignoring the Cheshire Cat, I looked around at the desolate barren landscape with a reddish hue that stretched for miles around us and wondered the same thing. Where are we?

Sherlock looked out at the terrain, examined the reddish soil at our feet, scrutinized it with his pocket microscope, sniffed at the air, stuck out his tongue and tasted it, and then slowly addressed us. "At least we are all alive for the moment, but for how long, I cannot guarantee. The local atmosphere of this place is very weak. Based on my work, *A Study of the Chemical Composition of Various Atmospheric Environments and Their Ability to Sustain Human Life,* it may not sustain us for very long. I am afraid with so many different minds influencing the Time Machine at the same time; we overloaded its functionality and standard operational process. We completely bypassed the time travel limitations maintained by the Time Guardians. It seems that the machine took us to the last thought that went through H. G. Wells' mind before we disappeared. Fellow travelers, we are on the planet Mars."

A stunned silence fell over our group, and the White Rabbit with his ears completely dropping tried to hide beneath the seat of the device. "I was only trying to help." he whispered. "M-M-Mr. Wells had said we were out of

58

time, so I thought I had to do something. The Time M-M-Machine seemed to be the only answer."

"Something, yes. But not launch us clear off the planet, my cute and cuddly friend," voiced the Cheshire Cat. "You could have at least sent us to the moon where we would have had some green cheese to eat. How are we to prevent Wonderland from disappearing from way out here?"

The Hatter quivered and seemed to be shrinking into his oversized hat as he pointed a shaking hand toward the horizon and proclaimed, "I am not quite certain or sure, as is typical, but Wonderland may be the very least of our problems. What is that tripod-looking thing coming this way?"

Off in the distance, a tall three-legged machine was striding towards us. It was a gigantic, metal mechanical walking device with three articulated legs attached to a central pod or body that had flexible mechanical arms extending from each side of it like the tentacles of an octopus. I had never seen anything like it before. It was intimidating in the least. One of the arms seemed to be holding a separate device of some kind. I was wondering what it could be when a beam of intensely bright light burst from it and scorched a furrow into the ground not too far from us. The device fired a second time striking even closer to our group.

Sherlock quickly took control of the situation declaring, "Well, that answers the question of whether or not the natives are friendly here. They most definitely are *NOT!* Unicorn, Jabberwocky, can you do something about that machine?"

The Unicorn reared up on its hind legs striking a regal pose for just a moment and then raced straight towards the Martian machine, stopping in plain view directly in front of it. It struck the ground in front of the tripod with its hooves as if to say, "Here I am you mechanical monstrosity. Try and catch me!" The Martian aimed and fired its heat ray weapon, but the Unicorn had already vanished from the spot and was taunting the machine from the other side kicking at the tripod's mechanical legs. The machine turned and tried to follow the Unicorn, firing its weapon wildly, but as I have already described, the Unicorn was so incredibly swift that the there was no possible way that the machine could catch it or focus its beam weapon on it

The heat ray flashed to the left and to the right ripping scorch marks across the Martian terrain as it tried to fire at the Unicorn to no avail. While the machine's occupants were focused on the Unicorn, the Jabberwocky swooped down on it from behind and grabbed the heat ray device in its claws, struggling with the tentacles for control of it. The Jabberwocky finally gained control of the device and turned it back towards the central body of the machine. The heat ray sliced directly through the center of the machine, and the tripod crumpled to the ground with a loud crash.

Unfortunately though, during the struggle for control of the weapon, the Jabberwocky had received a wound from the heat ray. As he returned to the ground in front of us, I could see the bloody laceration. I was at a complete loss as far as what to do, as I didn't have my medical bag with me. Not to mention I had no experience treating Jabberwockies. The Unicorn however raced up to the

Jabberwocky and laid its spiral horn directly on the wound. There was a soft silver glow, and within seconds the wound had completely healed.

"That was amazing!" I exclaimed. "What a doctor you would make!"

The Unicorn replied with a sideways shake of his head saying, "No thank you. I make a much better Unicorn. Not to mention, I get the attention of all the fair maidens and princesses. But I do have to be careful these days. Unicorn hunters have started to use fair maidens to try and lure me into traps. I really need to be cautious of that."

Sherlock applauded the Unicorn and Jabberwocky saying, "Excellent work! Now we must get off of this planet before any more of these things show up."

I agreed and pointed out that it had better be quickly, as it appeared there were two more of them over near the horizon coming this way. Off in the distance, I could see them as they quickly clanked their way towards us making great strides with their long mechanical legs. The two new tripods came to a sudden stop when they saw the destroyed remains of the first machine. They seemed to be assessing the situation and communicating between themselves.

Sherlock explained to our group, "If we somehow travelled to Mars by overloading the Time Machine's operating system, then I deduce that it is only logical that we should be able to return home by doing the exact same thing again."

The Martians, meanwhile, had come to some sort of conclusion about the situation and had begun deploying a new and different weapon. This one was a long metal tube that fired a grey canister a great distance from where they stood. The first canister fired fell short, but it burst into a dense black smoke cloud that quickly spread over the terrain in all directions. It curled and bubbled as it crawled out across the Martian ground. I wasn't certain what it was, but somehow I knew it was deadly. I pointed at it and advised, "That does not look very healthy at all. It's probably some type of poison gas. We have got to get out of here."

Sherlock hurried back over to the Time Machine, sat in the passenger seat, turned on the controls and directed us. "There is no time left. Everyone quickly, I want all of us to touch this machine together, and as I push the lever forward, let us all think of home. Ready? *Now!*"

Chapter 11. Yet Another Very Strange Side Trip (But not unexpected all, things considered.)

Sherlock thrust the lever forward, and once again, the air around us exploded into a burst of light and color. It felt like I was inside a giant kaleidoscope that was being rotated in a whirlwind. The motion was horribly nauseating. It seemed as if the Time Machine also was weakening under the strain of transporting all of us at the same time. It creaked and groaned while the disc whirled madly away. Just as I thought I could no longer stand the motion, Sherlock finally pulled the lever to a stop, and the machine came to a halt on what looked like the remains of a giant chess board surrounded by a field with a large red castle off in the distance. In unison, the five Wonderland inhabitants cried out together "Home!"

I looked at Sherlock in disbelief. While Holmes and I had both thought of Wells' home, the rest of them had thought of their home in Wonderland, and there were five of them compared to the two of us. I imagine it was an honest mistake. Sherlock really should have been clearer in his instructions. You know what they say: '*Always be precise in your directions.*' But we were under a great deal of pressure at the time with the additional Martian tripods approaching us and that nasty looking black smoke weapon.

"Are we r-r-really truly home?" The White Rabbit questioned as he looked around in disbelief. "Is it still here?"

"You all know that I am never really quite certain or sure about anything," replied the Hatter also looking all around. "But this time I think it may just be possible we are home again. What do you think Cheshire?"

Before Cheshire could answer, a shrill, shrieking voice from somewhere nearby cried out, "Off with their heads! *Off* with their heads! All of them, off with their heads! And be quick about it. I want to see some headway here."

The Cheshire Cat dematerialized his body, rotated his floating head upside down and replied, "Yes, I am quite certain that we are home. That must be the Queen of Hearts. I would know her screeching, caterwauling voice anywhere. And I am not talking about cats on the wall. Her voice makes bag pipes sound positively sweet and finger nails on a blackboard sound absolutely soothing."

Sherlock expressed a note of surprise. "Why that is a remarkable coincidence, I published a detailed study on *An Annotated Comparison of Bag Pipe Music to Finger Nails on a Blackboard Focusing on All the Major and Minor Keys in 4/4 Tempo.* By the time I had finished with that paper, I was able to play *Scotland the Brave* on a blackboard just using my finger nails. Isn't that just fascinating? I am surprised, though; no one really wanted to hear me play it."

We all then turned to look in the direction of the shrill voice and saw a column of oversized playing cards sporting human heads, arms and legs come marching towards us at a quick pace. They were dressed in red and white displaying the Hearts suit and carrying spears and halberds or other nasty looking medieval weapons. They did not look friendly at all.

At the back of their column, regally dressed wearing a ruby-studded golden crown, marched what appeared to be the Queen of Hearts. She was short and stocky, attired in a red and black playing card Hearts motif and carried a royal scepter. She looked less friendly than her army of playing cards.

"Who dares to trespass on the royal chess board?" she demanded. "There is so very little left of it there is no room for intruders, not even cute and cuddly rabbits. We shall have to have their heads for this. Guards, head them off, and then off with their heads. And remember, this time to use your heads. The last time you brought me heads of lettuce while you let the prisoners escape."

The White Rabbit's ears stood straight up and quivered when he heard "cute and cuddly" yet again, but most wisely, he refrained from saying anything. Drawing on his skills of observation, logic and deduction, Sherlock assessed the situation, boldly stepped forward and addressed the Queen: "Why, your Majesty, how could you think we are intruding when we are the chess pieces? We most certainly belong here. The rabbit in the blue coat is the pawn. The Unicorn and Dragon are the knights. This fine gentleman and I are the bishops. How dare you question us being here? It is you who are not prepared for a game of chess. Everyone knows that you don't play chess with a deck of playing cards. That would be almost as foolish as playing croquet with playing cards. If you persist in this folly I shall demand that you forfeit."

The Queen's face turned redder than her outfit. "What kind of nonsensical logic is that? How can you demand that I forfeit when it is obvious that I only have two feet?

Do I have to put my foot down here? You wouldn't have a leg to stand on. Not only that, you are being very impertinent. And what folly would you prefer me to persist in? The folly only runs twice a day and the morning folly has already left. Are you trying to derail this conversation? We must stay on track."

Sherlock firmly stood his ground and replied, "Your Majesty, if you are the Queen, then you can order a special folly any time you wish, to carry you anywhere you want to go. I am not suggesting that you get carried away here, but if we don't complete our task, then Wonderland and all of you will vanish forever. You would have no one to rule, and those are the rules. Trust me, you can ask the Time Guardians yourself."

The Queen hesitated for a moment looking rather perplexed and responded, "What are you talking about? I have never seen a time garden. I imagine it would be full of tics as well as tocs. Not to mention, the garden would be full of time flies. Why would anyone even give it a second thought? However, if as you say, there is not a minute to waste and the hour is at hand and as you said, since I am the queen, I can order a special folly. I hereby command a special folly." Then with a flourishing wave of her royal scepter she added, "Now!"

Much to my surprise, a vehicle looking something remotely like a trolley came clanging and banging in from the distance on tracks that somehow appeared on the ground in front of it as it approached us. When I say that it looked like a trolley, that is an exaggeration. It was more accurately something that looked like it might have wanted to be a trolley but could not quite make up its mind on the details of subject. It had wheels and seats and polished brass poles and most everything else a normal trolley would have, but none of them were where they belonged. It was as if someone took all the parts for a trolley car, mixed them up, threw them in a pile and they stuck together. It was a true folly.

The bizarre looking vehicle rattled up to us and screeched to a halt with its bell ringing the entire time. The Queen and her army of playing cards then boarded the folly. She gave a twirl of her royal scepter and commanded, "Off and ahead. Off and ahead!"

The trolley, or folly, or whatever you want to call it, clanged and banged its way "off and ahead" into the distance with the bell constantly clamoring until it faded away.

The Cheshire Cat reformed its body, smiled and sighed. "It's so good to be home and see that things are still on track. You certainly engineered a clever way out of that situation. That was using your caboose. When the Queen showed up with her army of playing cards, I thought the game was over for us all. That it was check mate so to speak. So what do we do next most logical and deductive one? Would you like me to catch a few time flies? They might possibly be able to help us return quicker and save some time."

The Hatter raised his hand, struck a public speaking pose, and pronounced, "I am almost sure you all know, that time flies like an arrow, but did you know that fruit flies like a banana."

The White Rabbit meekly responded, "And butter flies like a flower."

To which the Unicorn added, "Don't forget, horse flies like a barn."

The Jabberwocky concluded the discussion by interjecting, "And dragon flies like a knight. They are rather tasty you know."

Sherlock looked at the Jabberwocky and asked me if I had a Vorpal sword handy, to which the Jabberwocky replied, "I was joking, oh deep thinking and humorless one. I make no bones about it. That was in poor taste. I shall have to eat my words no matter how tasteless the comment. Might you have any pickled herring sandwiches to go with them? That would help immensely. Why I would be speechless with appreciation. Some tea would also help if you have any."

Sherlock shook his head, sighed and countered, "Watson, we have got to get out of this place before they drive me crazy."

Nodding in agreement, I turned to where the Time Machine had been sitting, but to my surprise and dismay it had vanished! It was nowhere to be seen! "Sherlock!" I exclaimed, "How are we to do that? Now the Time Machine has gone missing. And there are no signs of where it went."

Chapter 12. One More Very Strange Side Trip (And this time some talking flowers.)

Sherlock spun around quickly to see and verified that the machine was indeed gone. Where its battered remains had previously stood, there was nothing but an indentation in the ground.

Sherlock turned to the group and was about to speak when the White Rabbit held up his paws and loudly exclaimed, "It wasn't m-m-me. I didn't do it! Really I didn't. I was here in front of you the whole time. You can ask my watch."

Sherlock answered saying, "Don't worry, Rabbit, no one has said that you did anything *this* time. I want to ask, if any of you saw anything while the Queen of Hearts was leaving on the folly?"

In a panic, the group began answering in their typical fashion, of all of them speaking at the same time, starting with the Cheshire Cat shaking his head, "No, no, not at all."

Jabberwocky looking to the right and left repeatedly voiced, "I didn't see anything. Did you see anything? I really did not see anything!"

"But I wasn't looking in that direction," implored the White Rabbit.

In his speaking pose the Hatter declared, "I am not really certain or sure, and you know I am never really quite certain of *anything*, but I will say it certainly *looks* like it's gone."

"But how could it just disappear?" the Cat wondered while rotating its head. "Wasn't anyone watching it?"

The jabberwocky raised one claw and questioned, "Maybe it left on its own. Did anyone turn it off?"

The Cat reversed the direction of its spinning head, demanding, "How could it just *disappear*? I'm the only one that can disappear. Cheshire Cats can do that you know."

Dropping his gold watch, the White Rabbit slouched down to the ground with his ears and his whiskers drooping. "Now we are really out of time. We're doomed. We're DOOMED!"

The Unicorn then suggested, "Why don't we just follow the footprints?"

"Footprints? What footprints?" cried Holmes.
"Watson, you said there were no signs."

"Well I did not see any," I replied rather embarrassed. "I did not see anything useful. Why don't you come take a look? You're the detective. This is your area of specialization."

This entire mad tea party adventure was beginning to get to me. Normally I could handle Sherlock's superiority in everything related to his cases, but here nothing was as it seemed and everything seemed so strange and unreal. It was as if logic and common sense had been turned completely upside down. Yet, somehow Sherlock had still maintained his rational composure. How does he do it? Sherlock walked over to where the Time Machine had been standing and examined the area carefully. He took out his pocket magnifying glass, got down on the ground and studied certain areas with even more scrutiny. I watched him closely but could not detect what he was looking at, so I just waited until Sherlock stood up. "Well?" I finally asked him, "What did you find?

Sherlock stood there looking down at the ground and answered, "I am not quite sure yet. There are two distinctly clawed footprints that don't go anywhere and I am not at all surprised that they are not to be found in my *Complete Guide to the Identification of the Footprints of All Living Creatures on the Planet Earth.* It is obvious that a winged creature landed here briefly. Only long enough to snatch the machine and fly off with it. What it would want with the Time Machine, I have no idea, unless it wants the parts for its nest. It must be quite a large creature to be able carry off a machine that big."

Looking at the group of Wonderland inhabitants, Sherlock started to ask them a question but stopped, turned and looked at me and asked, "Do I dare?"

I shrugged my shoulders and replied, "Really, what choice do you have?"

Sherlock sighed, "You're right." slowly turned back to them and asked, "Would any of you happen to know what creatures here in Wonderland would be large enough to carry off the Time Machine?"

As was quite typical he received a multitude of wildly different answers.

"The Jubjub Bird!" whispered the White Rabbit looking fearful.

"The Griffon!" called out the Cheshire Cat. "He has wings and claws."

"I am not really certain, but you already know I am never really quite certain or sure of anything," offered the Hatter.

"We're doomed!" cried the White Rabbit.

"*The Jabberwocky*," stated the Jabberwocky quite straight forwardly.

When Sherlock gave him a puzzled look, the Jabberwocky countered. "YOU specifically asked what creatures in Wonderland *could* have carried off the Time Machine. I assure you that I am quite capable of carrying off that machine." He then twisted his long neck to stare directly at Sherlock. "I also assure you that it most certainly was not me."

He then withdrew his head from in front of Sherlock and proceeded to, one by one, examine his long, sharp claws.

Sherlock raised his eyes, shook his head back and forth and acknowledged, "Yes, Jabberwocky. Trust me. I am quite certain it was not you." Turning back to the group he asked, "Any more suggestions?"

"The Monstrous Crow?" offered the Hatter to which the Cheshire Cat replied, "Hatter, the Monstrous Crow has not been seen in Wonderland for ages. No one as seen him for quite some time, even before Wonderland residents started disappearing."

Finally the Unicorn suggested, "Could it have been the Bandersnatch? She is certainly capable."

"The Bandersnatch!" All the rest echoed at once, "Yes... the Bandersnatch. She is very frumious, most frumious indeed. It could very well have been Bandersnatch."

Sherlock looked at them and answered, "I am *so* glad that I asked. Who or what is the *Bandersnatch*?"

The White Rabbit raised a trembling paw, leaned forward, looked to the left and to the right, whispered in a low voice, "The Bandersnatch..." and promptly fainted.

The Unicorn, however, once again explained, "It is a fierce flying creature with very long legs, a long neck, and snapping jaws."

"Why that sounds almost like me." offered the Jabberwocky proudly.

Ignoring the Jabberwocky, the Unicorn persisted with his description of the Bandersnatch: "It is quite fast, but I assure you nowhere near as fast as I am. It is noted for being quite frumious, which is to say both *fuming* and *furious* at the same time. What it would want with the Time Machine I can't imagine."

Sherlock exhaled and stated, "If we are going to ever get out of here, we will just have to find out now, won't we?"

I was perplexed. "But how are we to follow it if flew away and there are no more than two footprints?"

The Jabberwocky flexed its wings and stated, "We don't need to follow it. If it went home, then we know where it went. Its home is in the Tulgey Woods not far from where I live. I can be there in no time at all."

The Unicorn, of course, replied, "In the time it took you to say that, I have been there and back several times. She is home in her nest, and so is our Time Machine."

"Excellent!" said Holmes. "Do you think you and Jabberwocky can get it back?"

The Unicorn shook its head, "That may be a tad problematic. I think you should come with us."

The Cheshire Cat, grinning widely as usual chirped in, "A 'tad' did you say? I know a swamp where we can find some tad poles if we need any. They are very useful if we need to vault any tads. That was an exciting event at the last track and field competition -- Tad Pole Vaulting -- almost as much fun as the High-and–Go-Seek Jump."

Needless to say, I didn't inquire as to what the "High-and-Go-Seek Jump" could possibly be.

The White Rabbit had regained consciousness, and Sherlock addressed the group. "Apparently, I will be needed in retrieving the Time Machine, so I have to go with them. Hatter, Rabbit, and Cheshire, if we leave you here, do you promise not to move from this place? We will be back as soon as possible and hopefully with the machine."

"I am absolutely glued to the ground," The Hatter assured us.

The eyes of the White Rabbit, however, grew very large, and he started quivering as he exclaimed, "You're leaving us?" At which point he again fainted and fell to the ground.

The Hatter looked at him and stated, "It doesn't look like he is going anywhere. And as I said, neither am I. My feet are *glued* to the ground. I think I may have stepped in some tree sap or something. My feet really *are* glued to the ground. I knew this would turn out to be a sticky situation. But don't worry, I will stick to it."

"Sort it out while we are gone, Hatter, and make sure the White Rabbit doesn't run off anywhere." Turning, he addressed the cat, "Cheshire, keep an eye on both of them if you please."

The cat grinned, blinked and snickered, "Well it's a good thing I have two eyes, since there are two of them. At least we are seeing eye-to-eye on this. I can't imagine how 'eye' would manage if there were three of them."

Sherlock turned to the Unicorn and asked, "Since you are so swift, can you take Dr. Watson and myself to the Tulgey Woods one at a time?"

At that point, I wasn't sure what was happening, but all of a sudden, it felt as if the Unicorn was materializing directly beneath me, picking me up on its back. I frantically wrapped my arms around its neck and held on for dear life as it took off like a bullet.

The few trees I was able to see in the blur I remember of that ride seemed to spring up in front of us and instantly vanish just as quickly. Several times, I shut my eyes fearing we were certain to crash into a tree. But before I could react, I found myself sitting on the ground near a forest, with the Unicorn and Holmes astride him standing nearby. The Jabberwocky was complaining to the Unicorn, "I really don't see why you got to give both of them a ride."

Sherlock motioned them to be quite and pointed towards the woods. In the branches of one of the trees was precariously perched the Time Machine along with numerous other loose branches, bicycles, brass beds, bits of old machines and other miscellaneous objects. Our machine was a part of a nest. Sitting in it was the Bandersnatch, a creature even stranger looking than the Jabberwocky, if that was at all possible.

The Bandersnatch had very long spindly legs and a long neck. Its wings were folded up so I could not see them well, but the claws and jaws that I could see were fearsome and ferocious. Its arms seemed to be of an average length, if there is such a thing for a beast such as that. The creature was a greenish-golden color that blended in well with the trees. Its eyes were purplish, and they darted back and forth as it continuously looked around the forest presumably guarding its nest. Somehow her eyes had a very sad and lonely look to them.

I looked at Holmes, the Unicorn, and Jabberwocky, and whispered, "Now what do we do?" I had envisioned an all-out assault on the creature in an attempt to get our machine back, but I was surprised when Jabberwocky took control of the situation, rising up and openly galumphing toward the Bandersnatch. Jabberwocky made a formal bow to the creature and addressed it in a burbling voice, "Greetings Lady Bandersnatch, most spindly and golden-green one. I bring you pleasant tidings this brillig and Frabjous day."

The creature's long neck and head spun swiftly towards the Jabberwocky and it answered sharply, "You mean you bring intruders here, you scaly, chortling beast. I see the other three with you. What are you doing bringing humans and a Unicorn here to my nest? No one comes here except to do me harm."

At that point, Sherlock stood up, walked towards it, bowed gracefully and spoke. "We mean you no harm, green lady of the woods. We are on an urgent mission to save Wonderland and all of its inhabitants including yourself. If we do not complete our task by the end of the day, this entire place and everything in it will cease to exist."

It careened its neck toward Sherlock. "Really? Is this true? How do I know you are telling the truth?"

I was going to mention Sherlock's famous paper on *Determining Whether or Not Someone is Telling the Truth by Observing Breathing Patterns, Eye Blinking, and Sneezing*, but I thought it best not to interrupt.

"And if you are telling the truth, what are you doing here instead of being somewhere else off saving Wonderland?

77

Either way, I think you should leave. You are intruding, and the only thing intruders want to do is run around swinging Vorpal swords and slicing off heads. No one comes here just for a friendly chat over a cup of tea. Go on. Off with you, or I shall have to get frumious. Trust me. You really don't want to see me when I am frumious."

At that point, the Unicorn elegantly stepped forward and gently addressed her. "Verdant creature of the trees, calm yourself. Be not concerned. I can vouch for this human and the other one as well. They have risked their lives repeatedly to save Wonderland and all of us in it. You *know* that Unicorns are completely truthful, and I say that everything he says is true and accurate. The reason we are here in Tulgey Woods is because our transportation device is somehow in your nest. We don't know how it ended up there, but we desperately need it back to complete our task to save Wonderland."

The Bandersnatch's eyes flared and her claws flexed. "Ha! I knew you were after something. They are always after something. A great number of odd and interesting things end up in my nest. Which object might be your transportation device?"

The Jabberwocky flapped its wings and rose to the level of the nest and pointed a long claw. "It is the brass and wooden device with the large disc on the back end. If you would return it to us, we would be happy to replace it with something else even more interesting and enjoyable."

The Bandersnatch recoiled its neck and head in surprise. "Do you mean you want to actually *give* me something? No one has ever given me anything before. That is why I collect odd and interesting things to keep me company.

78

Why various odd things find their way to my nest. Yes, yes, you may take it. It was in rather poor condition to begin with. If that pathetic thing is your transportation device, then Wonderland still may not have much of a chance."

The jabberwocky extended its claws and delicately snatched the device out of the nest and lowered it to the ground in front of Sherlock. It was fortunately not in any worse condition than before it had disappeared, which isn't really saying much, as it was just barely in one piece to begin with.

The Bandersnatch, with her eyes wide open, was really enthusiastic at that point. "All right, what are you going to bring me? I do love surprises, or at least pleasant surprises. You can't take the travel device until you bring me something. What do you have for me?"

I was at a loss for what to do next, as we didn't really have anything with us to give to the Bandersnatch. At that point, the Unicorn blurred, vanished, and then reappeared with an uprooted clump of brightly colored flowers held gently in its teeth. It pawed a hole in the ground directly in front of and beneath the nest of the Bandersnatch. There it delicately placed the flowers in the ground and carefully replaced the dirt around them. The Unicorn addressed the flowers encouraging them, "Okay, Snapdragons, welcome to your new home and your new friend."

The Unicorn looked up towards the creature's nest and called out, "Bandersnatch, come down and meet your new companions. You stated that no one ever comes just to talk or chat, so I knew you must be lonely. Here are talking Snapdragon flowers to keep you company."

The Bandersnatch cautiously descended from its nest to the ground and looked at the flowers quizzically. "Talking flowers?" she asked, "What a novel idea. Who would have thought of such a thing? It certainly isn't very logical. It sounds like something from a literary nonsense tale. The next thing you know, you'll be telling me that Time Machines really exist." Sherlock and I looked at each other and both of us decided not to comment.

The Snapdragon flowers took one look at the Bandersnatch and all cried out in unison, "Mummy!" and they all began talking to her at the same time. The Bandersnatch lowered its head to the ground in front of them beaming and was immediately lost in conversation.

Sherlock smiled and asked, "Jabberwocky, can you transport our machine back to the rest of the group while Unicorn transports Dr. Watson and I?"

Who would have ever believed what had just occurred? I was ready to launch an attack on the fearsome creature, and we ended up leaving it engaged in conversation with a group of talking Snapdragons. It's no wonder they call this place Wonderland.

Now if only the three visitors whom we had left behind were still waiting for us, we would have been able to get back to the business of saving this strange and unusual place. As I was soon to find out, however, that was a very big "IF".

Chapter 13. A Very Strange Discovery
(And not surprisingly Sherlock had already written a paper on it.)

I will spare you the details of my second near instantaneous Unicorn ride other than to say that when the Unicorn dropped me off to go retrieve Sherlock, it took me over a minute before I dared open my eyes. To this day, I still have nightmares of near collisions with trees at speeds that you could not possibly imagine. When I finally did open my eyes though, the Rabbit, Hatter and Cheshire Cat were nowhere to be seen. What could have happened to them? We really weren't gone all that long. Jabberwocky had replaced the Time Machine exactly where it had previously been and was airborne looking to see if they were anywhere in the surrounding area. Sherlock was already on his hands and knees examining the vicinity for clues. It may sound odd, but imaginary or not, I was concerned for our missing travel companions.

"Have you found anything?" I asked worriedly. "Do you think they may have already vanished from Wonderland like all the others?"

Sherlock stood and looked at me. "Well they are definitely gone and not here, but they are not *gone* gone, if you know what I mean. You know, this really is exactly the phenomena that I addressed in my paper on *The Analysis and Classification of Transitory States Based on Observable Side Effects Upon the Surrounding Environment with Particular Emphasis on Rabbit Hair.* Since we have been here, Watson, I have discovered that when something or some creature disappears from

Wonderland, there is no trace of it whatsoever left behind. They are truly gone. But if you look closely, you can see here where the White Rabbit fainted and fell to the ground; there are still some of his white hairs present. If he had actually vanished from Wonderland, there would be no white hairs or any other evidence of his previous existence. If you understand what I am saying, he would be *completely* gone."

Sherlock moved slightly over to the left, bent down, and pointed at the ground. "The same goes for the Hatter. He had said that he had stepped in some tree sap and was literally stuck to the ground. You can see that the grass is torn away from where he had last been standing when we left them. If he had vanished, then the grass would not be disturbed. Wherever they went to, you will see blades of grass still stuck to the Hatter's shoes. It is all part of proper observation, Watson. I assure you that, while they are not here, they are definitely somewhere."

Standing up and moving back to where the White Rabbit had been laying on the ground, he bent down again and looked even closer. "And if you look very closely, you can see a slight indentation in the dirt on either side of where White Rabbit had been laying. That clearly indicates to me he was picked up by a very large claw. The Hatter was standing, which is why there are no claw indentions in the ground. But as I mentioned previously, the grass that was stuck to his shoes was pulled away and torn from the rest of the field. I am positive they were both picked up and carried away by a very large-winged creature."

"That would probably be the Jubjub Bird," the Unicorn offered. "He is a nasty one."

"What about the Cheshire Cat?" I asked Sherlock. "What do think happened to him?"

"Now, that is an entirely different situation. Since he can dematerialize at will..."

"Actually, I can dematerialize not just at 'Will', but at anyone I choose to, which by the way, is a very good thing. That Jubjub Bird really gave me the Willies." Much to our surprise, the Cheshire Cat suddenly faded back into view close to where Sherlock was standing.

"That was a very astute explanation, most observant and comprehensive one," the Cat grinned. "You explained it exactly as it occurred. Just a few minutes after you four left, the Jubjub Bird swooped down and snatched the White Rabbit and the Hatter from where they were and flew off with them in that direction."

He pointed a paw in the direction of the Queen of Hearts' Castle and went on: "I was able to dematerialize so I did, and the bird was not able to touch me. I believe that we may need to pay a visit to the Queen if we want our friends back."

"But why would she do that?" I wondered out loud. "I thought Sherlock had made it very clear; if we did not complete our task, then Wonderland, her Majesty the Queen, and her entire kingdom would disappear forever. She seemed to have understood when she left in the folly."

"Maybe she had a change of heart," suggested the Cheshire Cat. "For all of her playing card army and all that, she can be pretty heartless you know. There is no use having heart-to-heart conversations with her. She does whatever suits her. It's all in the cards, as they say."

"We will have to get them back," said Sherlock. "But we need to leave someone here to guard the Time Machine. We certainly don't want it to disappear again."

"Or we could all go together, and the Jabberwocky can carry it to the Queen's castle," I suggested. "That way when we retrieve the White Rabbit and the Hatter, we can all leave as soon as possible and get back to Wells' house so we can finish this madness."

"And continue with the previous madness?" the Cheshire Cat grinned widely. "It's really no use. We're all quite mad here."

"Actually, Watson, that is not a bad idea, if you do not mind carrying the machine again Jabberwocky." Sherlock asked as he turned to the creature.

The Jabberwocky, however, was beaming with pride. "Of course I don't mind. Did I not mention that I was more than capable of carrying the Time Machine when you first asked what Wonderland creatures were able to do so?"

"Excellent!" said Holmes. "Cheshire, can you ride in the machine with the Jabberwocky while Watson and I ride with the Unicorn to the Queen's castle? That is, without touching any of the machine's controls, of course."

The Cat vanished from where it had been sitting and reappeared floating just above the chair of the Time Machine. It gave a sly grin and nodded to indicate that it was in the Time Machine, but obviously not touching anything. "Why of course, most curious and cautious one. I would not even think of touching the controls. You needn't worry. I have everything under control or actually under me as I just happen to be floating above the controls. I can do that you know. We Cheshire Cats are noted for that."

I was not very enthusiastic about the idea of another high-speed ride dodging trees on the back of the Unicorn, but I knew we had to complete this as soon as possible, so I tried to prepare myself. I had just closed my eyes when I felt the Unicorn's close presence beneath me again. I experienced a whirling rush of wind and the notion of trees flying past me at impossible speeds, when I suddenly found myself standing on the lawn in front of the Queen of Heart's castle.

A croquet court was laid out on the castle lawn with nine playing card soldiers bending over acting as the wickets. The White Rabbit and Hatter were tied to poles on either side of the Queen of Hearts' throne, which seemed to be placed in the position of the starting post of one side of the croquet court. There was a sudden scrambling and shuffling around of the playing card wickets changing their locations after the Jabberwocky had set the Time Machine down, and it was somehow sitting at the exact opposite end of the court in the position of the other starting post.

Behind the Queen's throne perched a particularly vicious looking oversized bird in a vibrant red and white plumage. I was sure that this was the feared Jubjub Bird. I did not have a good feeling about this whole arrangement at all.

Chapter 14. A Very Strange Game of Croquet (Only Sherlock Holmes could have managed this one.)

Standing next to me were Sherlock and the Unicorn, and in front of her throne was the Queen of Hearts with a very angry expression on her face.

"I don't know who you are or what your game is, but I can certainly see that it is a foot. I have tried to keep you at arm's length, but I need to hand it to you, you certainly know how to keep ahead of the game. You stated that Wonderland and its inhabitants are disappearing, and you are absolutely correct. I am not sure how you managed to do it, but all of the hedgehogs and flamingos have simply vanished from Wonderland. Now how am I supposed to play croquet?" she screamed while gesturing wildly.

Pointing a finger at Holmes she carried on, "I am positive that you had a hand in this, so rather than take up arms against you, you have left me no other option than this. Whether you have the stomach for it, or not, I must put my foot down. It's quite simple. If you want your companions back alive, you will play this croquet game against me per the following two rules:

1. The first player to maneuver his or her imaginary croquet hedgehog, using imaginary flamingo mallets, across the court to the opposite post wins.

2. All shots must be accurately described by the player and conform to the Standard Queen's Rules of Wonderland Croquet."

The Queen turned and pointed to a nearby pedestal on which there sat a book that must have been at least twelve inches thick. It was titled, *The Standard Queen's Rules of Wonderland Croquet: Abridged Edition.*

"If you win, you get your friends back alive and you can all leave. If you lose, you and all of your friends remain here playing croquet until Wonderland vanishes and the game is over for good. Those are my rules."

What was she talking about? This was insanity. Every second we lost could spell the difference between life and death, or at least disappearing forever, for all of them, and she wanted to play imaginary croquet?

Much to my surprise, Sherlock walked to the pedestal, leafed casually through the pages of the huge rule book, stepped forward, took some imaginary back-and-forth swings of a mallet and said, "I accept your Majesty. But you should be aware that, in addition to having written my magazine article on *The Logic and Geometry of Lining up Croquet Shots for Maximum Efficiency,* I have also published an entire series on *The Manipulation and Coordination of the Sensory Perception of Imagined Physical Actions on a Playing Field with Particular Emphasis as it Pertains to the Game of Croquet.* I am so experienced in this, that I have played and won entire matches of imaginary croquet with my eyes imaginarily blind-folded and one hand imaginarily tied behind my back. Allow me to demonstrate."

Sherlock walked over to the Time Machine, which served as the starting post for his side of the court, turned to the Cheshire Cat, held out the up-turned palm of his hand, and stated, "A Hedgehog if you please."

The Cat, of course, made the motion of handing Sherlock a Hedgehog, which he pretended to hold up for the Queen to see. Sherlock bent over, placed the imaginary Hedgehog on the lawn, loosened up his legs and arms, performed an elegant backswing with, of course, the imaginary flamingo mallet, and followed through with his swing.

To my astonishment, as the imaginary flamingo hit the imaginary Hedgehog, there was a very unimaginary and audible sound of the two making contact.

"Ah Ha!" cried Sherlock. "It went right through the first two wickets, bounced off of that pebble in the court right there, proceeded to go through the third wicket, hit that clump of grass, reflected backwards off of it and lined up perfectly for the fourth and center wicket. I now have three shots available."

That was amazing and quite creative on his part. I was sure that Sherlock would have this nonsense wrapped up in no time at all. The Queen of Hearts, however, had other thoughts on the subject.

"Guards!" she called out, and the center playing card wicket quickly straightened up and was about to run off, when the Cheshire cat pounced on it and forced it back into a hoop position. Sherlock quickly made a backswing and swung his imagined flamingo, and again there was an audible clunking sound of it making contact with the imagined hedgehog.

"Straight through again," he calmly stated. "And this time that gust of wind, caused by the Jabberwocky's wings, has blown the ball back and to the left to place it right in front of the fifth wicket. Of course, that was perfectly legal per the rules; if you check *Section 3, Subsection 8.5, Paragraph 2 on Atmospheric Conditions and Effects of Wind Naturally Created or Otherwise.*"

"GUARDS!" the Queen screamed again, but this time even louder. "Do something!"

The fifth playing card wicket that had been caught off guard jumped up to the upright position and was going to spear Sherlock's hedgehog, when the Unicorn stepped in front of it, bent its head down, and with a sharp twist of its horn, knocked the spear well off into the distance where it impaled the side of a tree. The Unicorn pointed its glowing spiral horn at the playing card and asked: "Now would you like to end up in the same position as your spear, or have I made my point?"

The playing card wicket took one look at the Unicorn's glowing horn and immediately dove back down into the hoop position trembling as he did.

The Unicorn smiled at him adding, "Good choice. It would have been pointless to resist."

Sherlock, meanwhile, had taken his next shot and launched the envisioned hedgehog towards the fifth wicket; however, a wall of playing card soldiers had taken a defensive position in front of the wicket to prevent the hedgehog from getting past. The Cheshire Cat, not to be out done, came bounding towards their direction, leaped at them, and in midair dematerialized its body so it was just a head crying out, "Heads up everyone!" crashing into the left side of the row of cards and knocking them all out of the way.

"Excellently done, Cheshire and Unicorn," Sherlock nodded as he walked over to the new position of the fantasized hedgehog, which apparently had followed a perfectly curved furrow in the lawn that had been created by the Unicorn to place it directly in front of the last two wickets.

"*GUARDS!!!!*" screamed the Queen yet again. "I will have your heads for this!"

The remaining two playing card wicket soldiers struggled desperately to escape, but were firmly held in their position by the claws of the Jabberwocky, who smiled and casually voiced, "I do believe it is your shot, most accurate and croquet talented one. The path is clear." Sherlock was in the process of swinging his imagined flamingo for the final shot to end the game when the Jubjub Bird, with a hideously shrill scream and its claws viciously extended, came diving straight towards him.

"Look out!" I cried, but they were too far away, and I could not reach my service revolver quickly enough, so there was nothing I could do. I thought Sherlock was done for, when suddenly the Bandersnatch came swooping in from the opposite direction, grabbing the Jubjub Bird in mid-flight and flinging it out of the court and against the wall of the castle where it crumpled to the ground in a flurry of feathers. Sherlock was able to complete his shot, and he raised his arms in victory.

The Bandersnatch landed in the croquet court and congratulated Sherlock: "That was an excellent shot, most truthful and vouched-for one. I had just wanted to come by and say thank you again for my wonderful new Snapdragon friends. They are so delightful and that was most kind of you. I simply had to find you all to say thank you again. It looked like that bird-brained combination of nails on a chalkboard and a moldy feather blanket was going to interfere with your game, so I got rid of it for you. But then what can you expect from birds? They are so aggressive that one would think they were related to dinosaurs. And I am sure you all know how that turned out."

The White Rabbit and the Hatter both gave a loud cheer as an audible clink of a make-believe hedgehog struck the Queen's throne and their ropes fell to the ground, freeing them. The Queen of Hearts stepped forward, curtsied and, most surprisingly, in a very calm and formal voice stated, "I must congratulate you sir. That was an outstanding game of croquet. It would have even been great standing inside. In fact, you are certainly standing in good standing inside or outside. It was quite excellent, really. The best game I have had in years. You must come back sometime again for a rematch. It's the Queen's prerogative you know. It is in the rule book. You *do* have to return for a rematch." Sherlock bowed and replied, "Yes, I know. It's on page 753, paragraph 5, sub-section 2, *The Queen's Prerogatives on Rematches.* When my current task is through, I shall endeavor to return for a rematch. But I really must be going now, Your Majesty."

"Well, then be off with you!" she commanded. "And not just with your heads. All of you be gone!" And with that she turned and paraded towards her castle with the bedraggled remains of her playing card army following behind her. Sherlock, meanwhile, was thanking the Bandersnatch for showing up and assisting when it did.

"No problem at all," The Bandersnatch replied. "I was happy to assist, but I really must return home to the wee ones or they will be plotting who knows what kind of garden mischief."

With that, the golden-green creature took off, and we were finally, all of us together with the Time Machine again in our possession. At last we would able to go home, but would there be enough time left?

Chapter 15. A Very Strange but Much Nicer Journey (And what incredibly beautiful music!)

As we all gathered around the Time Machine, I pointed out that we really had to leave, but I also asked Sherlock whether or not he thought the device could handle one more trip. It was already in rather poor condition when we had first arrived. We had overloaded its capabilities twice, and it been carted all over Wonderland by the Bandersnatch and the Jabberwocky.

Sherlock looked over the Time Machine. The rotating disc was warped and scorched. The varnished wood had been cracked in several places, and some of the brass railings were completely bent out of shape. "We have no choice, Watson. We must return to H. G. Wells' home and then to our flat on Baker Street if we are to succeed. Now, if we can all focus on the very SAME place, the home of H. G. Wells, let us try this again."

As Sherlock started to sit down in the passenger's chair of the Time Machine to try again, a soft ethereal music seemed to surround us all. It filled the area and sounded like it could have been a harp or a flute, or perhaps both of them together, or even something else entirely, totally unidentifiable but still incredibly beautiful. I had never heard anything quite like it before. It had a celestial, Celtic sound to it and was most enchanting and mystical, filling me with a great sense of peace. I had no idea what it could have been."

"What *is* that music?" I asked "And where is it coming from?"

"In this place who knows," countered Sherlock looking all around.

The Unicorn held his head up high listening intently and answered, "I *know* who that is. That is Pixy Music. I would recognize that sound anywhere. She is the most musically gifted of all the Pixies and faire folk. Her music is quite beyond description. There is no one else like her. That is why they call her Pixy *Music*, because she literally *is* 'Pixy Music'. Isn't she just beautiful? There really is no comparison."

Sherlock closed his eyes, remained still and listened intently before he responded, "You know before today, I would have said that there are no such thing as Pixies, or Unicorns, or any of you really for that matter. But here we are, all together, and I have to say that is without question the most beautiful music I have ever heard in my life. My violin playing can never compare to that."

Under my breath I added, "Sherlock, your violin playing could never even *hope* to compare to that beautiful music. Your violin playing is more comparable to a cat being tortured on a rack."

Fortunately, he didn't hear me, but the Cheshire Cat did give me a particularly nasty look.

"Yes!" the Unicorn enthusiastically declared looking up in to the air in the direction of the music. "Yes, yes, and thank you sincerely. We are truly honored, Pixy Music. Thank you again."

The Unicorn turned to the rest of us with a smile and a warm glow emanating from him. "We are safe. Pixy Music will provide protection for our return journey to the home of Mr. Wells. She observed the condition of the Time Machine and knew that it would never survive the stress of one more journey. It would have completely failed and we would have been lost forever. She wove a song of protection around it with her music. Now we can safely go home." And looking at Sherlock, the Unicorn added, "That is, to the home of H. G. Wells, of course."

Sherlock roused himself as if from a trance, placed his hand on the control lever of the Time Machine and began."All right, one more time. Everyone think of H. G. Wells' home, and touch the machine now!"

He carefully moved the lever forward, and this time it was as if we were surrounded by a celestial choir of harps and flutes. The rainbow lights and kaleidoscope were there almost the same as before, but it was not as chaotic or violent. It was a much smoother trip as we floated, more than raced, through the cosmos. The home of H. G. Wells seemed to be materializing all around us. We were once again back in his laboratory, and Sherlock slowly reversed the lever to the stop position for the last time. When Sherlock released the lever, and we all let go of it, the Time Machine collapsed into a pile of wood, brass and wires, while the spinning disc rolled off into a corner and fell to the ground with a loud metallic clang.

H. G. Wells looked at the ruined remains of his Time Machine and frowned, "You certainly are hard on your traveling accommodations. Remind me never to loan you my carriage in the future." He then broke in to a cheerful smile and exclaimed, "Welcome back everyone! I am glad you are all home and safe it seems. Is everyone all right?"

As we stepped away from the debris of the destroyed Time Machine, I thought I heard the last echoes of the enchanting music that had protected us on our journey home. I looked up, smiled, and turned to Wells. "Yes, we are all fine, but you would not believe where we have been to."

The Hatter excitedly interjected, "I know I am usually never really certain or sure about anything, but this time, I am positive! We have been to MARS! Can you believe it? MARS! The Martians have giant mechanical walking tripods and heat rays and poison gas and maybe something even more terrible! They may even be planning an invasion!" At that point, with his eyes wide and shaking all over, he pulled his hat completely over his head, and the White Rabbit once again fainted. Wells, meanwhile, seemed deeply lost in thought while talking to himself, "Hmm, a Martian invasion with tripods and heat rays. What an interesting concept. I shall have to consider that as a possibility for a future novel: "The War of the Planets", or perhaps, "The War of the Worlds", or something similar to that. I like it."

We all returned to the tea room, much to the approval of the Unicorn and Jabberwocky. Sherlock and I apologized for the condition of Wells' Time Machine and told him everything that had occurred while we were away.

"Amazing!" Wells replied. "Just amazing! I will never look at the planet Mars in the same way again. And Wonderland as well, that was incredible. Considering all that you told me, it is perhaps better that the Time

Machine is destroyed. That way, it will never fall into the wrong hands. However, I am still reluctant to loan you my carriage."

Holmes stood up and shaking the hand of his host, said goodbye."Mr. Wells my dear sir, you have been most helpful, most helpful indeed. We must all take leave of you now and return to 221-B Baker Street. It is there that the final portion of this journey will begin. Where it will end depends on what happens next. Time is indeed of the essence."

Chapter 16. A Very Strange Brew (But really rather tasty.)

Hearing that Holmes had proclaimed the end of the gathering, The Unicorn proceeded to finish the rest of the tea, and the Jabberwocky emptied the last of the sandwich trays. The Hatter roused the White Rabbit, echoing, "Wake up Rabbit! It's time to go. Time is a-wasting. There's no time like the present. Let's be timely now. It really is about time," and other ill-timed comments.

Hearing that we were to travel again, the Rabbit threw himself at Holmes' feet pleading with him. "Please M-M-Mr. Holmes, no m-m-more air travel!"

Sherlock assured him that it might not be necessary, and in fact, it did not seem quite possible without a carriage, unless they could procure a replacement.

The Unicorn then pointed its glowing horn at an empty table, nodded its head once and asked, "Would these help?"

Suddenly there appeared on the table, several small bottles with little labels that said, "Drink Me!" Recalling Carroll's novel, I pointed to them and asked, "What possible use would we have for a growth potion?"

To which the Unicorn corrected me stating, "The 'Drink Me' bottles that were described in Lewis Carroll's novel were quite different than these 'Drink Me' bottles. If you recall, Dr. Watson, the bottles he described in his book had a red-colored liquid; whereas, the liquid in these bottles on the table is most distinctively lilac in color. I would think that even the most unobservant reader should be able to see that."

"That's wonderful!" I exclaimed. "What does the color of the contents have to do with anything?"

The Cheshire Cat reappeared, sporting a red and lilac striped pattern, saying, "Well that is a rather 'off-color' remark. I'm surprised it did not stick to your palate. Is that what you call 'purple prose'? I have 'red' about that you know."

Ignoring the Cat, the Unicorn went on with his explanation, "Why everything! The color of the contents is quite significant. As illustrated in Lewis Carroll's novel, red is indeed a growth potion. Lilac, however, is a transportation potion. You just say where you want to go, drink it, and your there. It's really quite simple."

"Do you m-m-mean to say we could have completely avoided those last trips?" exclaimed the White Rabbit, jumping up and down in front of the Unicorn. "I nearly broke m-m-my watch bouncing around in that coach. M-my ears m-may never be the same again and those Time M-Machine trips, they were almost unbearable."

The Cheshire Cat of course added, "Well it's a good thing we did not see any 'bears' while we were 'bear rolling' along."

The Unicorn shook his head. "No, not exactly, my cute and cuddly traveling companion. This potion only works when there is absolutely no other possible option available. And as the only other option available now is the Jabberwocky flying all of you there without a carriage, I would say now is the appropriate time to use it. There are five bottles on this table. Jabberwocky and I would not need one as we can travel nearly as fast as the potion."

"Faster, if we avoid the scenic route!" interjected the Jabberwocky.

To which the Unicorn replied, "I have been there and back five times in the time it took you to say that."

Holmes then declared, "If you two would table your debate for just a moment, we could already be there and moving forward. Now, everyone, except Unicorn and Jabberwocky, take hold of a bottle and open it. Now repeat *exactly* after me, '*221-B Baker Street, London.*' Now drink."

In the moment that followed, a number of things seemed to happen. I heard five voices somewhat in unison recite the address to our flat, or something that sounded somewhat close to it. (I do recall wondering if that would affect the final result or destination.) The strange brew that we had drunk smelled sweet and fragrant, like a bouquet of roses. It tasted something like vanilla, and going down, it had seemed almost like I was swallowing the thorns from the roses. Once I had swallowed it, I felt briefly as if I were melting, when suddenly I was back in 221-B Baker Street with the Cheshire Cat sitting on top of my head and commenting, "Well that was entirely better than being bashed about in the coach, and if I do say so, quite a quite bit quicker. Not as scenic though. It wouldn't sell nearly as many tour tickets."

The Jabberwocky, who was curled up in a corner,

commented that the speed was due to not having to take the longer sightseeing route that Unicorn used, to which the Unicorn replied, that he had made the round trip seven times in the time it took us to arrive.

Holmes looked around to verify everyone was present, but he came up two travelers short. A loud knocking on the outside of the window indicated that the Hatter had ended up outside on the window sill, and he was quite relieved to climb inside when we opened it. "As we left, I was almost, but not quite certain or sure that I got that wording correct, but then you know that I am never really certain or sure about anything," he explained to Holmes. "And I may have added an additional word or two about being left out on a ledge."

"You're here Hatter", admonished Sherlock, "That's all that matters. Now where is the White Rabbit?"

The answer to that question was to be heard in the bakery across the street in the form of loud crashing sounds accompanied by someone yelling something about, "Get out of the carrot cake! Get out of the flour! Get out of this shop right now! This is NOT a pet shop, no matter how cute and cuddly you are!"

We looked out the window to see the White Rabbit running at top speed out the front door of the bakery, leaving a set of floury white footprints, a stream of cooking utensils flying behind him, and a fading voice screaming, "That does it. Tomorrow I am moving to France! No one in this country appreciates a good bakery."

The Unicorn seemed to blur for a second and then clarified again, this time with the White Rabbit on his back clinging tightly. With a proud but casual shake of his head, the Unicorn announced, "It seemed to me, he needed some assistance out there. I told you I am very quick."

The Rabbit slid off of the Unicorn's back, landed at Sherlock's feet, and looked up sheepishly saying, "Really sir, I was quite certain that I heard you say *Bakery* Street."

Holmes ignored the Rabbit's comments and asked me to fetch Mrs. Hudson, stating that she would be required to participate in the next step of the proceedings. I did not have to go far, as she was just entering the room with a tray of tea and sandwiches for us when she suddenly stopped in her tracks and gazed about the room at the odd collection of creatures.

"My goodness! How very curious! Sherlock, Dr. Watson, I was going to tell you both about the most wonderful and strangest thing that happened to me today. I was quite sure that I had seen the briefest glimpse of a Unicorn in the garden several times earlier this morning, but here he is right here in your study. Can you imagine that? There is a Unicorn in your study? And yet somehow it does not seem nearly as strange next to all the rest of your guests. Goodness! You have such a darling cat, a cute and cuddly rabbit, and a dragon in addition to the Unicorn! Sherlock, I really don't think the pet policy covers *any* of this."

Sherlock approached her and explained, "Yes, Mrs. Hudson, I am quite certain that you did see a Unicorn in the garden earlier. Later on, I can hopefully explain it all, introduce you, and you can formally say hello to him and all the rest of my guests. But right now I need you to sit right here."

Sherlock took the food tray, set it on a table, sat her in a chair, and then arranged us into a circle with chairs for everyone except the Unicorn and the Jabberwocky. The right half of the circle consisted of the Hatter, Mrs. Hudson, and me; while the left half of the circle included the Cheshire Cat, the White Rabbit, and the Jabberwocky. Sherlock had the Unicorn stand in the center of the circle while he slowly and contemplatively walked around the creature addressing us.

"Friends, I must ask you to maintain your position in this circle and not to say a word, or even move while I concentrate. If this works as I expect it to -- and I am not often wrong -- I may seem to vanish from your perspective, but do not be alarmed. It is imperative that you do not move, or you may disrupt the field that I create. Unicorn, with your permission, I will sit on your back while you stand in the center of the circle. If my deductions are correct, and I am certain they are, this arrangement will open the portal for me to travel to the reality outside of time."

We agreed, wishing Holmes the very best of luck in his endeavor. Naturally, he responded by saying, "Luck has nothing whatsoever to do with this. Even with all of the strange things we have experienced today this is still one hundred percent logic and deduction, of which I am the master."

"Well then, the very best of logic and deduction," the Hatter offered.

The Unicorn bowed low to allow Holmes to climb onto his back and returned to the standing position with Holmes sitting astride him. Sherlock looked around the circle at each of us, and with a long deep sigh, closed his eyes and whispered; "Now it begins."

Chapter 17. A Very Strange Conflict (Just what exactly is going on here?)

I must confess that, at the time, I honestly did not expect much of anything to happen. I mean seriously, what could possibly have happened by having the group of us sitting around in a circle while Holmes sat there and concentrated? Yes, it is true that he was sitting on a real-live Unicorn, and it had been a somewhat unusual morning what with the talking cat and all, and there were those trips to both Wonderland and Mars, and we were in the physical presence of several imaginary creatures from a children's novel. A dragon had provided not one, but two, air trips between London and Guildford, and we had been somehow instantaneously transported to 221-B Baker Street by drinking a potion provided by a Unicorn. There was that incredible imaginary game of croquet, not to mention the Bandersnatch and the talking Snapdragons. Now that I think about it again as I write this, considering everything that had happened up to that point, I can't imagine why I had any real doubts.

But at the time, I did have doubts, many real doubts. What was Sherlock's plan? Why were we arranged in a circle? Why had he requested Mrs. Hudson to be a part of it? What did she have to do with the proceedings? Did any of this make any sense at all? Why don't I just get up, go out and have a nice relaxing breakfast and forget about all of this nonsense? It is probably just a bad dream or something. Yes, that's it. It is a very bad dream. I will just get up, walk out the door, go have a nice normal breakfast without talking cats and rabbits. And when I return, Sherlock will be sitting in his chair, puffing away on his pipe, or be at the table deeply involved in some arcane odd-smelling experiment. I will mention to him what a strange and curious dream I just had, and he will dismiss it completely, and we will laugh, move on, and never talk about it again. That was the right answer, to get up and just walk out the door.

As these and other questioning thoughts drifted through my mind, I suddenly felt a presence, as if another consciousness was in my mind along with me. A great sense of peace came over me similar to when the Unicorn had first laid its horn upon my shoulder. After that, I could have sworn that I heard its warm voice again, repeating its message to me: "Believe Watson, just *believe!*" I was also sure that once more I heard the enchanting and peaceful Pixy Music that I had heard when we took our final time-travel journey. It seemed to faintly fill the area with its ethereal hypnotic sound.

I redoubled my efforts and focused on the group, focused on the Unicorn, and focused on Holmes sitting on the Unicorn. I even focused on focusing. I cast aside all the questions and doubts and tried to truly see whatever it was that Holmes was seeing. As it turned out, I thought I was starting to see things when Holmes and the Unicorn suddenly became blurry and less focused. They somehow looked less solid, as if I was seeing them in a nebulous dreamlike environment.

They appeared to be standing in a river. A river was right there in our study in 221-B Baker Street! A RIVER! How could that be? As I watched them in their dreamlike state, they slowly stepped out of the river on to the shore, and the vision abruptly ended. I found myself staring at an empty space in the middle of the circle. We all looked at the empty space, and then each other, then back at the empty space. After that we waited. No one said a word. No one moved. We just waited.

We all knew that Holmes had said to remain in the circle until he completed his task and solved the logic puzzle, but how long would that take? When would he be back? Would he be able to return? Could he even solve the ultimate enigma of logic? What would happen if he failed? What would we do then?

Wait a minute! Of course he would solve it. What was I thinking? This was Sherlock Holmes I was talking about. He is, without question, the master of perception, deduction and logic. I knew better than to think that he could fail. It was as if my mind was a battlefield of conflicting thoughts. A part of me had complete and total confidence in him, while another part of me wanted to run away and never look back. I felt like I was mentally under attack. In looking at the expressions of the others gathered in that circle, I saw similar mental conflicts going on in the rest of us as well. The White Rabbit was nervously glancing back and forth from his watch to the center of the circle while his ears twitched wildly. The Hatter was fidgety and looked like he wanted to shrink into his hat and hide. The Jabberwocky's long slender claws were tapping the floor impatiently as if it wanted to tear something into shreds. And the Cheshire cat seemed to be straining to stay solid and not just fade completely away.

Mrs. Hudson, however, seemed quite serene and as peaceful as if she were out for a stroll in the garden. She had a sparkle in her eyes and a soft, gentle smile on her lips that almost seemed to say, "Everything is just fine. I know Sherlock has it all under control. All we need to do is wait. When he returns, we will all have some tea and cakes. I must be sure and get some cream for that darling little cat and some carrots for that cute and cuddly rabbit. I wonder what Unicorns eat? He is such a handsome creature. And what on earth will I give to the large scaly beast over there?" Her peaceful demeanor, complete confidence and total acceptance of the odd situation gave me strength. I was able to push away the doubts and fight back against all the nagging questions. I breathed deeply and sat up straighter in my chair. I looked to my companions and tried to silently convey my renewed energy and belief in Sherlock's ability to resolve the situation. He was the master of logic and deduction. There was no mystery or puzzle on Earth, or Mars, in Wonderland, or anywhere else for that matter, that Sherlock could not solve, and anything the Time Guardians came up with would be mere child's play to him. I envisioned my confidence radiating out to the group and to Sherlock as well just to be safe.

As I did, I noticed the Rabbit seemed less nervous and not as concerned with his watch. The Cheshire Cat followed by growing more solid and less translucent. At that point, I would have sworn that I had heard the Unicorn's voice saying, "Yes, Watson, you are doing it. Don't give up now." The soft strains of the comforting Pixy Music grew stronger and clearer. Feeling more confident, I resolved to focus all of my strength on supporting Sherlock in whatever he was doing, wherever he was doing it. I could see by the posture of the rest of the group they were also feeling a renewed strength. It was as if in one mental voice we were saying together, "Sherlock, we are with you!"

At that very point, the room faded away as if I was

waking up from a dream, and in its place as clear as day, was a river. Standing next to the river on a green and wooded shore were Sherlock and the Unicorn. In front of them, clothed in long flowing robes, stood the Guardians of Time.

Chapter 18. A Very Strange Game of Logic (But my bet is still on Sherlock.)

The three Guardians were tall slender beings, each in a different color robe. One was in white, one was in grey, and one was in black. Their facial features were entirely hidden by hoods, and they appeared to be as motionless as statues. Standing nearby, frozen as if in a three-dimensional photograph, were Lewis Carroll and a young girl in a blue and white dress. I was certain that she must have been Alice. Off in the distance I could see the Walrus and other characters from Wonderland.

I was amazed! Holmes had really done it. He had actually reached the very moment in time that the Guardians had given life to Wonderland, Alice, and all the rest of its inhabitants. He had reached the lost beginning that Carroll had mentioned in his letter.

A cold, ethereal voice emanated from the direction of the Guardians, "Your terms are agreeable, Sherlock Holmes. If you can solve all of the logic puzzles we put forth, Wonderland and the lives of all of its inhabitants will be spared. But if you fail, Wonderland, as well as you, will vanish forever. It will be as if you never existed. Let the contest begin!"

I was shocked! Had I heard what I thought I had just heard? Sherlock had wagered his very life on his ability to solve the ultimate logic puzzle. Even Lewis Carroll had not been able to solve it. What would happen if he failed? What would we do then? My thoughts were interrupted as the first Guardian stepped forward and spoke.

"Sherlock Holmes, I am the first Guardian. You may call me Cryptic. Here is your question. What is greater than God, and more evil than the Devil? The poor have it in abundance while the rich need it, and if you eat it, you die?"

Holmes replied almost immediately, "Nothing. Nothing is greater than God or more evil than the devil. The poor generally have nothing, while the rich most certainly need nothing, as they typically have everything they want. And if we eat nothing, we will most definitely die."

The Guardian nodded his head and stepped back.

The second guardian stepped forward, stood for a moment, and spoke, "I am the second Guardian. You may call me Logic. Sherlock Holmes, your reputation as a great detective has reached us even here in the realm outside of time. You might say that your reputation is timeless. We have a crime for you to solve. A certain timepiece has gone missing and there are six suspects. Here are their statements. We know without question, that exactly four of the statements are lies and the rest are all true. Here is what they have said:

Suspect A said:
It wasn't B.
It wasn't D.
It wasn't E.

Suspect B said:
It wasn't A.
It wasn't C.
It wasn't E.

Suspect C said:
It wasn't B.
It wasn't F.
It wasn't E.

Suspect D said:
It wasn't A.
It wasn't F.
It wasn't C.

Suspect E said:
It wasn't C.
It wasn't D.
It wasn't F.

Suspect F said:
It wasn't C.
It wasn't D.
It wasn't A.

Who is the guilty suspect?"

Holmes tossed his head back, laughed and stated, "You gave me the answer yourself. It is suspect 'C'. If it were any other suspect, then there could not be exactly four false statements."

The second Guardian nodded and stepped back replying, "That is quite correct."

The third Guardian stepped forward and spoke, "I am the third Guardian. You may call me Rubic." He opened up his hand in which there appeared a small cube that consisted of many smaller cubes in a 4x4 array. That is, four squares long, by four squares high, by four squares deep. As he held it up for Sherlock to see, the stack of smaller cubes remained quite solid as if they were all glued together. Each of the six faces of the main cube was a different solid color, being red, yellow, blue, green, black, and white, so that on any given side, all of the smaller cube faces were of that one color.

"This is my cubic challenge. You will note that I am able to rotate the individual faces of the cube, while the cube as a whole stays intact." He rotated one entire face of the cube 90 degrees so that the colors of the smaller squares had changed position, and the individual faces of the main cube were no longer all the same solid color. He proceeded to quickly rotate the rest of faces until all the smaller cube faces on each of the six main faces of the cube became a jumble of different colors. Handing the cube to Sherlock, he stated, "Your task is to return the cube to its original state of each of the six faces being a solid color. You have fifteen minutes. You may begin."

A large hour glass, which I know did not hold an hour's worth of time, suddenly appeared suspended in the air next to the guardian. Much to my frustration, Sherlock spent the first five minutes just staring at the cube. He examined it first from one side and then from the other. Sherlock turned the cube back to the first side, and once again on to a different face.

Why wasn't he doing something? I could see that he was mentally working out the nature and details of it, but time was flowing past with each gurgling splash of the river next to us and with each grain of sand that fell through the hour glass. When was he actually going to start returning it to its original state? Another five minutes of inaction went by, and I could almost stand it no more. I was about to break silence and yell at him to do something already, when he suddenly burst into action and started rotating the faces of the cube so rapidly I could not follow his movements. The colors of the cube became a rainbow blur as he rotated the faces first this way and then that way. I could see the intense focus in his eyes while the hour glass seemed to be emptying much faster than it should have been. It was a close race between the grains of sand and Sherlock. I was certain that he would solve it, but the question was, could he do it in time? Just as the final grains of sand were draining from the top of the hourglass, Holmes returned the final face of the cube to its original position, gave a long, deep sigh and held up the cube completely restored to its original state. With his wry smile he handed it back to the third Guardian saying, "That was actually quite exhilarating. You know, I believe there could be a future in marketing this thing as a toy or a puzzle. Of course it would be just for fun and pleasure and not as a contest with one's life or the fate of a whole world at stake."

I almost detected a smile in the hidden face of the Guardian as it retrieved the cube from Sherlock, nodded and stepped back adding, "Indeed it does, Sherlock Holmes. The future does hold much greatness for this device when it finally appears in your world. You could even write an article on solving it. I imagine it would be called, *Using Logic Based Movement Patterns and Three-Dimensional Rational to Solve Rotational Color Grid Cube Puzzles.*"

The first Guardian again stepped forward and spoke, "Long ago, a king was inspired by the concept of truthfulness. He decreed that everyone in his kingdom must always and without fail speak the truth. Anyone who did not speak the truth would be executed, and everyone who did speak the truth, no matter what he or she said, could not be executed. The proclamation was written out and posted at all of the gates to the kingdom. Guards were also posted to make sure everyone who entered the kingdom knew the rule and understood it under penalty of death. "One day a traveler approached the gates of the kingdom and the guards informed him of the proclamation and asked the traveler, 'Why have you come here?'

"His response was, 'Why, to be executed of course!'

"The guards apprehended the traveler and said, 'Oh, we have such a liar here. Let us take him to the king to be executed.'

"They brought the traveler to the king to be executed per the royal proclamation, but he was released. Why?"

Sherlock dismissively replied," It is obvious, of course. If he had been executed, then he would have been telling the truth, and per the proclamation, they could not execute him for telling the truth. They had to let him go."

The first Guardian again nodded and stepped back, as the second Guardian once more stepped forward.

"In addition to logic puzzles we also enjoy athletic competitions as well. We recently watched two foot races, a 100 meter race and a 200 meter race in which the same four contestants competed.

"Contestant 3 beat Contestant 4 in the 200 meter race.

"Contestant 1 came in 3rd in the 200 meter race.

"The 16-year-old won the 200 meter race.

"Contestant 3 came in second in the 100 meter race.

"The 15-year-old won the 100 meter race.

"Contestant 1 beat the 18 year old.

"The 19-year-old came in 3rd.

"Contestant 2 is 3 years younger than contestant 4.

"The contestant who came in last in the 200 meter race came in 3rd in the 100 meter race.

"Only one contestant finished in the same position in both races.

"Tell me the ages of each contestant and what position they finished in each race.

"You have five minutes."

Once again, the hourglass rotated while Holmes stood there silently staring at the Guardian. How was he supposed to solve the problem without a notebook or something to write on and put things in order? I could not even remember all of the statements much less determine who was who or how old they were and what position they finished in both of the races.

While I was starting to worry about the outcome, Sherlock seemed unconcerned. His eyes darted back and forth as he appeared to be mentally moving the various factors back and forth. The hourglass was not even halfway finished when he addressed the second Time Guardian. "Here is your answer. I believe you will find it completely correct as this is the only logical conclusion:

"Contestant 1 is 15 years old and finished 1st in the 100 meter race and 3rd in the 200 meter race.

"Contestant 2 is 16 years old and finished 4th in the 100 meter race and 1st in the 200 meter race.

"Contestant 3 is 18 years old and finished 2nd in both races.

"Contestant 4 is 19 years old and finished 3rd in the100 meter race and 4th in the 200 meter race."

The second Guardian bowed his head and responded, "Very good, Sherlock Holmes. Once again, you are correct."

The third Guardian named Rubic again stepped forward. He raised his hand and made a curving downward sweeping motion. "Your logic skills are most excellent, Mr. Holmes. You have been appointed as the facilitator in a crucial peace negotiation between representatives of five warring tribes. Each tribe has sent two representatives to the meeting. It must succeed or all is lost.

"Your task is to get all of them to the other side of a river to the meeting site for the negotiations. They have all previously agreed that once they are on the other side of the river, that they will not be hostile to one another. In addition, while in your presence as the facilitator, they will refrain from all violence. However, if they are left alone on this side of the river, violence most certainly will break out between them based on any and all of the following conditions:

1. The first tribe will attack members of the fourth tribe.

2. The second tribe will attack members of the first and fifth tribe, but only if both of the second tribe members are present.

3. The third tribe members will attack the first and fifth tribe member, but only if there is just one of them present.

4. The fourth tribe members will not get in the boat with the third tribe members.

5. The fifth tribe members are cannibals and will attack any one left alone.

6. The boat will only hold five people at a time, so you may presume that multiple trips will be required.

"Be careful whom you leave with whom, Mr. Holmes. This is no easy task. It is imperative that they all get across the river alive.

"My question is, how do you propose to get them all across the river safely so that the negotiations can be successfully completed? They arrive in two minutes."

Two minutes! How in the world was Sherlock supposed to accomplish this task? The fifth tribe members will kill anyone so they would have to be taken first. Who should he put in the boat with them? He would have to take one of the second tribe members since they both need to present to attack anyone. Who would be the fourth person he would put in the boat? The conditions made it nearly impossible as far as I was concerned. There is no way he could transport them all across the river without someone getting killed. Could he wait until they are all asleep and then bring them over? But what if one of them wakes up while Sherlock was in the boat crossing the river? That would be disastrous. He could possibly tie them all up, but again, if even one of them managed to escape, it will be all over. How is he going to solve this? I watched in wonder as Holmes stood there in silence analyzing the information.

Sherlock raised a hand pensively and asked the Guardian if those were *all* the rules to this puzzle. I did not understand why he would have asked that particular question, as the rules already given seemed more than difficult enough to me. I would have considered it impossible as is.

Rubic tilted his head under the hood and replied, "Yes, those indeed are all the rules. What do you propose Mr. Holmes?"

Sherlock's answer was simple."Swim. That's right, just *swim*. There is no *requirement* to use the boat. Every one of them swims across the river along with me at the same time. We don't use the boat at all. No one is left alone with another tribe member. No one gets attacked. They all reach the other side at the same time alive and safe, and the meeting can begin. After we all dry off, that is."

The three Guardians spoke in unison. "Well done, Sherlock Holmes. You have completed the basic logic riddles and have reached the final logic puzzle. This is the ultimate logic puzzle. It is the enigma. Your life depends on your ability to solve it. Do you wish to continue? You are aware that if you fail to solve it, you will forfeit your life. Or would you care to just go back home to your study on Baker Street with your Earthly friends who have been observing you and forget about Wonderland and all of its inhabitants? If you leave now, we will let you live, but Wonderland and everyone it, will vanish forever from the memories of your world. You will not remember it. It will be as if it never existed. This is your final chance."

Sherlock gazed around as if he could actually see us gathered in the invisible circle that surrounded him. He smiled and said simply, "I am ready for your ultimate logic puzzle."

Chapter 19. The Ultimate Logic Puzzle (And of course a very strange one at that.)

The Guardians bowed their heads and then all three took a step forward together. There was a shimmering in the space next to them, and an open scroll entitled "The Rules" suddenly appeared suspended in the air as if it was hanging from some invisible post. Sherlock stepped up to the parchment and read it aloud.

"The Rules:

"The three of us, Cryptic, Logic, and Rubic, are from this point forward, and in no particular or predictable order, True, False, and Random. True will always speak truthfully, and False will always speak falsely. However, it is a completely random matter whether Random replies truthfully or falsely to any given question. Your task is to determine which of us is True, which of us is False and which of us is Random by asking only three Yes-No questions. Your questions may only be put to only one of us at any given time.

"As you are well aware, we do understand English, but for the purposes of this challenge, we choose to answer all questions in our own language in which the words, *yes* and *no* are *ney* and *niy* in some order, but not particularly that one. You must solve this puzzle in one hour."

The hourglass rotated so the sand was on the top again, and the three Time Guardians in one cold, calculating voice said, "You may begin."

What had Sherlock gotten himself into? This was no puzzle. This was shear madness! He was only given three yes-no questions. They wouldn't answer in English, he didn't know their language, and one of them couldn't even be relied on to give consistent or correct answers. This was insanity! How could he ever have been expected to solve this in the time period given?

Lewis Carroll was an absolute master in logic puzzles, and he had been working on it for years without having solved it before he passed away. How was Holmes supposed to solve this puzzle in less than an hour? I was not alone in my concern, for I observed the same uncertainty in the others seated around Holmes and the Unicorn.

The Cheshire Cat was again starting to look less solid, and, for the first time since it had appeared, was not grinning. The Hatter, meanwhile, was again fidgeting and seemed to be shrinking into his oversized hat. Looking towards the Jabberwocky, I was certain I saw smoke curling from his nostrils as he nervously tapped the ground with his razor like-claws as if he was thinking, "Let me at them! Just let me at them, and I can solve the puzzle in no time at all by simply tearing the Guardians into little, tiny pieces. No Guardians, no puzzles, no problem!"

I gave him a stern look that clearly said, "Don't you even think of moving! You heard what Sherlock said. We must hold our position. If we break the field that is maintaining his presence here, you know that all is lost, and all of this would have been for nothing. If anyone in the world can figure out the answer, I know that Sherlock Holmes is the one person who can solve it." I hoped I had convinced him, since I was still so uncertain myself. Looking in the direction of the White Rabbit, his ears and whiskers were drooping worse than ever. He had lost all interest in his watch and looked as if he might faint at any moment. I hoped he could hold himself together, as each and every one of us was needed to maintain the circle.

Of all of us, only the Unicorn and Mrs. Hudson seemed at ease. She sat there serene as could be, a picture of complete and total confidence in Sherlock Holmes, the incredibly talented, yet certainly odd, lodger she had come to know so well over the years. His eccentric behavior of shooting bullet holes in the wall, creating foul smelling experiments, smoking noxious pipe tobacco, seeing strange visitors at all hours, and playing his screeching violin at 3:00 A.M. had not unnerved her after all this time. So in her mind, what was a simple, albeit incredibly complex and near unsolvable, question on which rested the entire fate of Wonderland and even Sherlock Homes himself? If anyone could solve it, Sherlock Holmes could. It was as simple as that!

The Unicorn was also the very essence of peace and serenity. Like a majestic ivory statue it stood firm and resolute and a silver glow emanated from where it stood. I heard the gentle calming sound of the mysterious Pixy Music once more as well. There appeared to be a warmth about the whole area that enveloped us as Holmes stood lost in deep concentration. The ancient eyes of the Unicorn slowly glanced around the members of the circle, and I could see and feel each of us strengthened by its gaze as it passed over us. When it had finished looking upon us, it turned its gaze to Sherlock, looked at him with an intensity that defied description, and I would have sworn that Holmes himself was almost glowing.

As I gazed upon Sherlock who was lost in concentration and deduction, I could only wonder what was going on in his analytical mind. The puzzle was certainly beyond my deductive capabilities. So many times before, Holmes had commented on how obtuse I was in matters that were as clear as daylight to him. He would explain his observations and conclusions and amazingly they would somehow seem quite simple and obvious. That was his way. That was Sherlock Holmes, but while I was sure that he could solve it, the question in my mind at that moment was could he solve it in time? The sand raced through the hourglass as Holmes stood there in complete silence staring at the scroll that hung suspended next to the Time Guardians. While there was no question that the sand was quickly disappearing, I saw a confident smile on his face that told me everything was going to be all right. With a smile, Sherlock started nodding his head, as if he was mentally working an equation, moving factors back and forth, this way and that way. Finally, Sherlock sighed, turned to the Guardian identified as Logic, and spoke with a voice that was as clear as a crystal and as deep as time itself.

"Here is my solution. I shall put forth my logical deductions and resulting conclusions for each possibility, and you will see that I have solved your puzzle:

Starting with you, Logic: if I asked you the question, 'Are you Random?' in your current mental state, would you say *niy?*
If you answer *niy*, you are indeed Random.
I would then ask Cryptic: If I asked you 'Are you True?', would you say *niy?*
If Cryptic answers *niy*, then Cryptic is True and Rubic is False.

If Cryptic answers *ney*, then *Cryptic is* False and Rubic is True.
In both cases, the puzzle is solved.

However if you, Logic, answer *ney,* then you are not Random.
I would then ask you: If I asked you 'Are you True?', would you say *niy*?
If you answer *niy*, then you are True.
If however you answer *ney,* then you are False.

I would then ask you: If I asked you 'Is Cryptic Random?', would you say *niy?*
If you answer *niy,* then Cryptic is Random, and Rubic is the opposite of you.
But if you answer *ney,* then Rubic is Random, and Cryptic is the opposite of you.

"Gentlemen, ladies, or whatever you may happen to be, that is my answer. If my deductions are correct, which I am certain they are, that is the only correct solution."

The silence was resounding as Holmes finished presenting his solution. The hourglass sand had first froze mid stream and then abruptly vanished along with the hourglass. The three Guardians stepped backwards one step, bowed as one and replied, "You have, indeed solved our ultimate logic puzzle, Sherlock Holmes. It is one which has never before been solved. To be completely honest, we were not even certain that it ever could be solved. However, in examining your deductions and conclusions, we see that they are correct. You have won the restoration of Wonderland and all of its inhabitants, as well as saved your own life. We shall now retire to our contemplations to create a new logic puzzle worthy of us.

Congratulations to you and your associates. You may all leave."

With a grand sweep of their arms, the Guardians, the river and the wooded shore disappeared, and the in the next moment, we were back in our flat in 221-B Baker Street. Somehow, even Lewis Carroll and Alice were there along with us. I was about to congratulate him, when a tea cup went flying past my head, crashed into the wall, shattered into pieces, and the White Rabbit loudly exclaimed, "How wonderful! Even the M-M-March Hare is here!"

Sherlock looked closely at the pieces of the shattered tea cup on the floor and proudly exclaimed, "Hah! Exactly per my calculations in *Quantifying the Number of Pieces Tea Cups Will Break Into When Thrown against a Wall Based on the Material Composition and Density of the Tea Cup.*"

Chapter 20. Yet One More Very Strange Tea Party (And a most pleasant conclusion.)

Looking around and seeing that all of us had safely returned to our Baker Street parlor brought me an immense sense of relief which was unfortunately quickly shattered by a loud roar, crashes, and screaming coming from the bakery across the street. I looked out the window to see the baker and several patrons come racing out the front door of the bakery screaming something about the zoo keeper should be fired for not containing the animals and the baker was definitely leaving the country for anywhere that did not have zoos.

They were quickly followed by a golden colored-lion, wearing a tweed vest and spectacles and a walrus sporting a monocle. The Unicorn suddenly appeared on the sidewalk in front of 221-B gesturing with his horn towards our front door, to which the Lion and Walrus quickly made their way. The Unicorn reappeared in our flat, which was already somewhat crowded, what with the Jabberwocky and everyone else, when the door opened and in squeezed the Lion and Walrus, greeting everyone as they did. "Hello there," saluted the Walrus. "Good evening. It is nice to meet you. Whoops, sorry about your foot there good fellow."

The Lion gave the Unicorn a friendly hug. "Unicorn, my old sparring partner, it is good to see you again. My, what a cute and cuddly rabbit you have here! Well, those are lovely looking tea cakes. Might you have any plum cake to go with them?"

"Gracious! What a large kitty cat!" exclaimed Mrs. Hudson, as the Lion paraded past her. "Would you like some milk? And perhaps some pickled herring sandwiches for your Walrus friend?"

The Jabberwocky quickly straightened his neck, picked up his head, nearly taking out a ceiling light fixture, and ventured, "Did I hear something about pickled herring sandwiches? What a lovely idea! Can I help you? I could go fetch a whole net full of fish from the wharf if you would like." He started to move forward, almost upsetting the coal scuttle and a stack of papers when Sherlock intervened, "Jabberwocky, why don't you just stay in one place for now until we get everyone settled. Things are just a bit crowded at the moment, but I am quite pleased to see all of you here. I can finally say that we were successful. Wonderland is saved."

At that point, the little girl in the blue and white dress stepped forward, curtsied and spoke, "Hello, my name is Alice. I was on my way to Wednesday-afternoon tea with Rabbit, Hatter and Cheshire Cat, when I somehow seemed to have gotten lost. I don't remember exactly where I was. Now I see that either I am found or everyone else is lost along with me. I can certainly tell that this is not Wonderland. In fact, this looks a great deal more like London, except that so many of my Wonderland friends are also here with me. I really don't understand it at all, but since we are all together, why don't we have the tea party right here? It would make it so much more fun. May I help with the tea in any way?"

"I'll help too!" cried the March Hare, flinging another tea cup across the room. This time, instead of crashing into the wall, the cup was expertly caught by Lewis Carroll, who snatched it out of the air and then handed it to Alice, who then went with Mrs. Hudson and the Hatter to get refreshments. Lewis Carroll smiled and exclaimed, "My dear friends, it is so wonderful to see you all again and to know that, thanks to Sherlock Homes, you won't disappear and be forgotten. You will live forever, not just in the hearts of readers around the world but in Wonderland itself! It is saved! Thank you, Mr. Holmes. Thank you ever so much! And thank you too, Dr. Watson, and the rest of you as well. I wonder though, how you managed to do it. How *did* you manage to step out of the river of time?"

"First things first!" cried the Hatter as he, along with Mrs. Hudson and Alice, reentered the room carrying trays with tea, sandwiches and cakes. "I am never really quite certain or sure about anything except tea time, so I am most pleased to say, it's TEA TIME!" Once everyone was settled in with their refreshments, although it was a mite crowded, we sat spellbound as Sherlock spoke.

"The first thing I want to say is that I discovered something most curious today. *Reality* really is relative. During my entire career as a consulting detective, I have focused on the consistency and importance of trifles that are invisible to most everyone else. I have relied on this unseen reality being both consistent and logical. I had mentioned to you earlier, Watson, that in this adventure, we were dealing with a whole different set of rules of reality. If you recall, it was about the time that the Unicorn walked into the room. That was the key to understanding what to do and how to do it. That is why I arranged you all in circle to gain access to the reality outside of time. But I am getting ahead of myself. And I will have no heady remarks from you sir," he added looking in the direction of the Cheshire Cat.

The Cat's grin widened as it replied, "Why I was not going to say anything about 'Heads' up! Here comes a good story because Sherlock Holmes used his 'head'." Then it winked at Sherlock, rotated its head completely upside down, and winked out, only to reappear sitting on the fireplace mantel, where it added, "Please do go ahead."

Shaking his head sideways, Sherlock went on, "As I was saying, by the end of the first two hours of the Cat's presence, I realized that the previous rules of logic and reality were no longer valid. As strange and improbable as it seemed, this was a whole new reality with a new set of rules. That was the only logical answer. From that point forward, it was a matter of adapting to the new reality. With each new event, regardless of how strange it was, deducing how to proceed became easier and easier, almost elementary."

The Cat grinned brightly and interjected, "Is that like a tree that only grows the twelfth, thirteenth, and fourteenth letters of the alphabet? I saw one of those once, a real L, M, N tree."

Sherlock paused for just a moment as if he were going to say something, raised his eyes to the ceiling, sighed, and then turned to Lewis Carroll. "I do want to say thank you, Lewis, for your clue regarding H.G. Wells. I knew that due to your agreement with the Time Guardians, you couldn't divulge more detailed information regarding the methodology for stepping out of the river of time, but Mr. Wells was able to provide exactly what I needed to know. That was an extremely clever clue. Even Watson, who has spent years observing me, did not notice it."

I looked at him and emphatically stated, "Sherlock, as you have said many times before, no one has better skills in observation and deduction than you. You should know that by now."

"That is true," he matter-a-factly acknowledged. "That is quite true, but while your deductive abilities may be sorely lacking, your insights and efforts in keeping the circle together and focused while I was in conflict with the Guardians was of immense help. We each have our own forte, Watson. I am truly glad you were there."

Sherlock turned back to the whole group to continue his story. "H. G. Wells was able to give me enough information about what I needed to do, so that I was able to devise a logic-based mental construct for stepping out of our reality. I do wish he was here so I could thank him."

At that moment, the Unicorn blurred slightly, vanished, and then reappeared with a bewildered looking H.G. Wells astride him and clinging desperately on to his neck. "Well why didn't you say so?" asked the Unicorn, as Wells dismounted and slid down to the floor, still somewhat shaken by his near instantaneous ride. The Unicorn proudly stated, "There is room for one more, as long as we all don't inhale at once. What is it, Sherlock, that you want to say to Mr. Wells?"

Holmes put out his hand to Wells saying, "I want to thank you again for explaining the dimensional time travel process. As you can see, it worked, and we managed to save Wonderland. By arranging a circle with humans sitting on the right side and imaginary creatures sitting on the left side, I created a balance of logic and illogic. It was a balanced combination of fact and fantasy, so to speak.

131

The Unicorn's ability to travel anywhere instantaneously gave me the ability to jump out of our reality. And those of you that comprised the circle provided the right balance of energy with which to do so and remain there. I really must write a paper on this someday. I think I will call it *Achieving Inter-Dimensional Travel Through the Balancing of Real and Non-real Beings Based on their Logical Placement in a Circular Arrangement, Focusing on Travel outside of Time.*"

Sherlock turned and addressed Mrs. Hudson directly: "I knew there would be a great strain on all of us, which is why I wanted to include you, Mrs. Hudson. Your calm nature and complete confidence in me helped the others to maintain their courage."

Mrs. Hudson replied with a shy smile, "Why thank you Sherlock. That is most kind of you, but it still does not mean I approve of your violin playing at three A.M., your foul smelling experiments, or the bullet holes in the wall."

Sherlock coughed twice and turned to the Unicorn, "And Unicorn, your strength and encouragement to all of them, as well as to me, was felt and very much appreciated."

Sherlock then paused for a moment with a far off look in his eyes and added, "That includes you as well, Pixy Music, wherever you are. You held the Time Machine together long enough for us to get home. We could not have done this without you." At that moment, an echoing musical laughter drifted through the room and touched us all, leaving a sense of peace and calm.

As the echo softly faded away Holmes resumed. "I am proud of all of you for not giving in to the mental attack

132

that the Guardians launched against you. I know it was quite a struggle. You realize, of course, that had the strength of the circle failed, I would have failed and we would have lost everything."

Humming loudly "*Will the Circle be Unbroken*", the Cheshire Cat, with an extra wide grin, stopped his tune and interjected, "Oh, I would not say that, most logical and victorious one. I am sure you would have gotten 'around' to it someday, perhaps when we are all more 'well rounded' on the subject. I will say this, however, the mental attack felt like a choir of out-of-tune accountants singing the multiplication tables backwards in Pig-Latin. It just did not add up."

Sherlock looked squarely at the Cat, which vanished from the mantel and reappeared in the ceiling light fixture, adding, "Do go on, Mr. Holmes. Things are 'looking up' right now."

Resuming, Sherlock explained, "Once I reached the reality outside of time, I knew it was just a matter of observation, deduction, and rational thought to solve their puzzles. As long as the circle held and I could remain there, I knew I could do it. Their initial puzzles were really quite elementary, but I will say, however, the final puzzle was certainly a challenge."

"But how did you solve that one Sherlock?" chimed in Lewis Carroll. "I was close to solving it, but I literally ran out of time."

Sherlock nodded his head, "I mentally created a 16 x 16 grid to map out all possible answers and variations. I reduced it to three logical connectives, or biconditional questions. It could have been solved in two questions if the first guardian had turned out to be 'Random'."

Looking intensely at Holmes, the Jabberwocky raised a claw and bowed its head saying, "If you don't mind, most deductive and victorious one, I will pass on that game of chess for now. Even without wings, you are at a level far above me."

Holmes bowed his head to the Jabberwocky answering, "That is fine with me, most scaly and aeronautically gifted one. Whenever you would like to have that game, it would be a pleasure and an honor to play a game of chess with you. Until then, you may want to take a look at my monograph on *Practical Applications of Deductive Logic and Rational Thought Process in Chess Openings Focusing on the First Three Moves.*"

Lewis Carroll then stepped forward, offered his hand to Sherlock, and stated enthusiastically, "Holmes, that was brilliant, indisputably brilliant! I applaud you!"

"Me too!" cried Alice, clapping her hands. "I'm not sure I understood any of those big words, but it did sound most impressive, and best of all, we are not lost anymore."

Reaching for the curtains to blow his nose, the Hatter piped in, "That is so very touching. I think I am going to cry," but he was intercepted by Mrs. Hudson who handed him a tea towel and gave him a most stern look that said, "Now see here, I can deal with rabbits, cats, lions, walruses, Unicorns and even dragons in the tea room, but don't you even think about using my curtains as a handkerchief."

The Hatter accepted the tea towel from Mrs. Hudson and blew his nose, this time sounding something like a large frog croaking through a rusty, barnacle encrusted fog horn.

The gathering broke up into smaller groups as we each discussed our own parts in the incredible adventure, with many verbal jousts between the Unicorn and Jabberwocky regarding who was really the fastest. They eventually agreed that the Jabberwocky was the fastest winged creature in the room, while the Unicorn was, without question, the fasted four-legged creature.

Finally, Lewis Carroll stood and looking at the clock stated, "My time on earth, which as you all know has already passed once, is again coming to an end. I have to leave now, but this time I can go in peace knowing that Alice, Wonderland, and all of the rest of you are safe. Thank you. Thank ..." He never finished his sentence. He just faded away before our eyes. In a twinkling he was gone, and Alice buried her head in Mrs. Hudson's arms to hide her tears.

Sherlock stepped over to Alice, bent down, put his hand on her shoulder, and in the gentlest manner that I have ever seen displayed in him, Sherlock addressed her, "Don't cry, little one. Lewis Carroll will with be with you in every Wonderland adventure you have from this day forward. He is the father of Wonderland, so to speak, and he is never far away from you. His spirit will live on in Wonderland forever."

Alice looked up at Sherlock, and her tiny smile broke into a grin, and she replied, "Really? Really? Then lets all go play Wonderland croquet!" She jumped up, grabbing the hand of the Hatter and the paws of the White Rabbit and March Hare, laughing out loud, "Let's go Cheshire! I bet I can beat you this time!"

In an echo of laughter, she was out the door with her friends following her and the head of the Cheshire Cat floating along behind calling out, "Farewell all! It has been great fun and most curious. Do let me know if you are ever in the mood for some illogical musing or mewing, whichever you don't prefer least!"

The Lion, followed by the Walrus, exited with many thanks and also saying, "See you soon Unicorn. Tomorrow we will continue our sparring match. Be sure and bring some plum cake. I will bring the brown bread."

And with that, the only ones that remained were Wells, Holmes, Mrs. Hudson and I plus the Jabberwocky and the Unicorn. They were discussing who should take H.G. Wells back to his home in Guildford and were about to get into another debate when Holmes interrupted, "Gentle creatures, Mr. Wells has already enjoyed the incredible privilege of riding upon a Unicorn so it is only fair that Jabberwocky should be the one to provide him the return trip to Guildford. He has yet to experience the wonder of air travel. It really is quite amazing, you know. He may even find inspiration for another novel, Flying from the Earth to the Moon, or perhaps The First Men inside the Moon."

"I like the idea of men inside the Moon," Wells commented. "I could really do something with that. I think that Jules Verne fellow has already written about a journey around the Moon and back. He imagined firing them out of a cannon of all things. And why would he put the launch site all the way over in Florida in the United States of America?"

"Wonderful!" exclaimed the Jabberwocky. "That sounds excellent! I think Mr. Wells will really enjoy the trip, as long we don't have to follow the Unicorn."

While Wells and the Jabberwocky said their goodbyes and left, I saw Holmes talking quietly to the Unicorn and the Unicorn nodding its head in agreement, but I could not hear what they were saying. Holmes and the Unicorn together walked up to Mrs. Hudson and Sherlock addressed her. "Mrs. Hudson, earlier I promised you that if we survived this adventure, I would personally introduce you to this amazing creature. Well, Mrs. Hudson, it is my great pleasure to introduce you to the Unicorn. And Unicorn, this is my dear Mrs. Hudson."

The Unicorn then bowed low on his front legs and said, "Dear gentle lady, it is truly a pleasure to meet you. Have you ever wanted to ride upon a Unicorn?"

The biggest smile imaginable shone on Mrs. Hudson's face as she embraced the Unicorn and climbed onto its back. Glancing in my direction and seeing my concern, the Unicorn winked at me, "I do promise I will go much slower this time." Then as the Unicorn exited the room, I heard it call out. "Good bye, gentlemen. Always remember, I was the fastest."

We heard a faint echo that sounded like the Jabberwocky from somewhere outside and far above saying, "But I fly faster..." followed by another echo that sounded like the Unicorn saying, "But I'm still the fastest...."

Once they were gone, we returned to our chairs and sat in absolute silence for quite some time. I looked around the empty room and then at Sherlock and with a sigh stated, "Well, Holmes, I guess it is over. That was, without a doubt, the strangest most curious adventure we have ever had. I absolutely must record it, but as you mentioned earlier, I certainly cannot publish this right now. I must postpone its publication. Who would ever believe me? They would think I was crazy! Tell me Holmes, am I crazy? Did we really travel to Mars? Did we actually visit Lewis Carroll's Wonderland? Did any of this really happen? Or did we imagine all of it? I mean, what proof do we have that any of this ever occurred?"

Holmes looked at me intensely and pointed in the direction of the door replying, "Turn around Watson. Your answer is right behind you."

I quickly turned around only to see Mrs. Hudson come waltzing back through the doorway, flowers in her hair, and a childlike smile that was almost glowing. As she lightly danced passed us, she laughingly stated, "Sherlock, that was absolutely wonderful! You needn't worry about the pet policy anymore. You can invite your friends over whenever you would like."

In a twinkling she was gone, but I could not help but smile. "Well, Holmes, I guess I can see now that it really did happen. Amazing! I wonder, do you think we will ever experience another adventure as truly strange and curious as this one?" Before he could answer, there was a knock at the door and a tall bearded gentleman in some type of navy blue uniform entered and asked, "Is this the residence of Sherlock Holmes?"

Holmes looked the gentleman over, nodded his head and answered, "I am Sherlock Holmes. How may I help you?"

Removing his hat, the gentleman responded, "My name is Captain Nemo of the submersible vessel the *Nautilus*. I would like to engage your services to locate a missing person. His name is Jules Verne."

The End

References:

1. Alice's Adventures in Wonderland, Lewis Carroll 1865

2. Through the Looking Glass, and What Alice Found There, Lewis Carroll 1871

3. Alice in Orchestrailia, Ernest La Prade 1926

4. Alice's Journey Beyond the Moon, R.J. Carter 2004

Also from MX Publishing

MX Publishing is the world's largest specialist Sherlock Holmes publisher, with over a hundred titles and fifty authors creating the latest in Sherlock Holmes fiction and non-fiction.

From traditional short stories and novels to travel guides and quiz books, MX Publishing cater for all Holmes fans.

The collection includes leading titles such as _Benedict Cumberbatch In Transition_ and _The Norwood Author_ which won the 2011 Howlett Award (Sherlock Holmes Book of the Year).

MX Publishing also has one of the largest communities of Holmes fans on Facebook with regular contributions from dozens of authors.

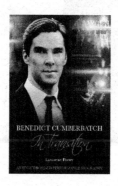

www.mxpublishing.com

Also from MX Publishing

Our bestselling short story collections 'Lost Stories of Sherlock Holmes', 'The Outstanding Mysteries of Sherlock Holmes', 'Untold Adventures of Sherlock Holmes' (and the sequel 'Studies in Legacy') and 'Sherlock Holmes in Pursuit'.

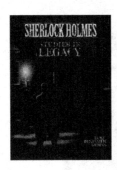 

www.mxpublishing.com

Also From MX Publishing

London, 1920: Boston-bred Enoch Hale, working as a reporter for the Central Press Syndicate, arrives on the scene shortly after a music hall escape artist is found hanging from the ceiling in his dressing room. What at first appears to be a suicide turns out to be murder . . .

(the first in the Sherlock Holmes and Enoch Hale trilogy)

www.mxpublishing.com

Also from MX Publishing

Lego Sherlock Holmes

Seven original adventures from Sir Arthur Conan Doyle,
re-illustrated in Lego.

In this book series, the short stories comprising The
Adventures of Sherlock Holmes have been amusingly
illustrated using only Lego® brand minifigures and bricks.
The illustrations recreate, through custom designed Lego
models, the composition of the black and white drawings
by Sidney Paget that accompanied the original publication
of these adventures appearing in The Strand Magazine
from July 1891 to June 1892.

www.mxpublishing.com

Also from MX Publishing

"Phil Growick's, 'The Secret Journal of Dr Watson', is an adventure which takes place in the latter part of Holmes and Watson's lives. They are entrusted by HM Government (although not officially) and the King no less to undertake a rescue mission to save the Romanovs, Russia's Royal family from a grisly end at the hand of the Bolsheviks. There is a wealth of detail in the story but not so much as would detract us from the enjoyment of the story. Espionage, counter-espionage, the ace of spies himself, double-agents, double-crossers...all these flit across the pages in a realistic and exciting way. All the characters are extremely well-drawn and Mr Growick, most importantly, does not falter with a very good ear for Holmesian dialogue indeed. Highly recommended. A five-star effort."
The Baker Street Society

www.mxpublishing.com

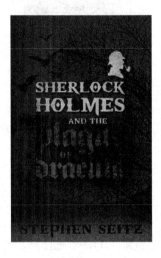

CPSIA information can be obtained
at www.ICGtesting.com
Printed in the USA
FSOW04n0539051016
25630FS